Mr. McAllister
Sets His Cap

Mr. McAllister
Sets His Cap

Laura Paquet

THORNDIKE
CHIVERS

This Large Print edition is published by Thorndike Press®, Waterville, Maine USA and by BBC Audiobooks, Ltd, Bath, England.

Published in 2004 in the U.S. by arrangement with Zebra Books, an imprint of Kensington Publishing Corp.

Published in 2004 in the U.K. by arrangement with the author.

U.S. Hardcover 0-7862-6533-7 (Romance)
U.K. Hardcover 0-7540-9647-5 (Chivers Large Print)

The text of this Large Print edition is unabridged. Other aspects of the book may vary from the original edition.

Set in 16 pt. Plantin by Myrna S. Raven.

Printed in the United States on permanent paper.

British Library Cataloguing-in-Publication Data available

Library of Congress Cataloging-in-Publication Data

Paquet, Laura Byrne, 1965–
    Mr. McAllister sets his cap / Laura Paquet.
      p. cm.
    ISBN 0-7862-6533-7 (lg. print : hc : alk. paper)
    1. Dwellings — Maintenance and repair — Fiction.
2. Scots — England — Fiction. 3. London (England)
— Fiction. 4. Home ownership — Fiction. 5. Architects
— Fiction. 6. Widows — Fiction. 7. Large type books.
I. Title.
PR9199.4.P366M7 2004
  813'.6—dc22   2004041275

Mr. McAllister
Sets His Cap

One

"Mr. McAllister is an excellent architect, Em, and most pleasant to deal with. I know you will enjoy working with him." Clarissa Carstairs, Countess of Langdon, sounded utterly confident — as she had all her life.

And — as she had almost all her life — Emily Wallace, Viscountess Tuncliffe, wished she had one-tenth of her younger sister's backbone.

"I am certain I will," Emily said, trying to sound definite. "You have spoken favorably of the work he did on your conservatory in the country."

"After I introduce you, would you like me to stay to help negotiate?" Clarissa's husband Matthew asked. "Since we have worked with him before —"

Emily cut him off before she could be tempted to accept his offer. "That is so kind of you, but I really must learn to do these things myself, if I am to live as a widow of independent means." She laughed at the funny little phrase. It had come to her as she had been tidying up her despised marital home in Hampshire,

Tuncliffe Manor.

Her late husband Simon had done precious little to provide for her — in fact, he had done his best to use up every cent of his inheritance and her dowry. The only reason she now had "independent means" — however meager those means were — was that a fall from a horse had snapped Simon's neck two years ago.

Emily admonished herself not to think such irreverent thoughts. Simon might not have been the most exemplary husband in England, but she should respect his memory. After all, he was the last husband she ever intended to have.

"You can easily manage this negotiation with Mr. McAllister," Clarissa said. "After all, you put up with Simon for five awful years."

"Clare —" Emily began.

"Yes, I know. No mocking the deceased. I promise I will be quiet." Clarissa pinched her lips closed with her fingers, then giggled, spoiling the effect.

"You see what I must deal with?" Matthew asked his sister-in-law, rolling his eyes. "Heaven help our poor child, with a madwoman for a mother."

At the mention of the coming baby, Clarissa and Matthew shared an intimate smile. While Emily rejoiced for them, a tiny, mean part of her spirit cracked each time she witnessed their excitement. She had wanted a baby so much, but God had not seen fit to bless her and Simon with a child.

What was bedeviling her today? She had to stop thinking about the past and start focusing on the future. And the first step would be getting her new house in habitable shape.

She rose from the cream-colored Grecian chaise, one of the items Clarissa had recently purchased to put her stamp on Stonecourt. Her sister had a flair for decorating; Matthew's London home had become a much warmer place since her arrival.

Emily had enjoyed her extended visit with the Langdons, one of several sojourns she had spent with them since Simon had died. Over the last two years, she had moved from relative to relative while putting her affairs in order, since she had had no home to call her own. Now it was time to settle down. And to do that, she had to find an architect.

"Shall we move to the library to await Mr. McAllister?" she asked Matthew. "He should arrive any moment, and I would like some time to collect my thoughts before he arrives." She took a deep breath and smoothed her suddenly damp palms down the skirt of her simple muslin day dress.

"Remember, Em, if it does not seem feasible to repair Simon's town house, you are always welcome to make your home with us," Clarissa said.

"I know that, and thank you," Emily said, leaning down to give her sister an impulsive hug. "But, I must admit, I am most curious to find out whether I will enjoy having my own establishment. Imagine! I shall be able to decorate as I wish, rise when it suits me, eat what I like and stay up reading until dawn if it so amuses me."

"No one deserves her freedom as much as you do," Clarissa replied. "And I know that Mr. McAllister will be able to redesign that decrepit old town house in no time. If you are clear about your budget, he will do his best to work within it. You must simply be firm."

Firm, Emily repeated to herself as she quit the room and preceded Matthew down the corridor toward the Langdons' imposing library. She must stand on her own two feet during these negotiations. It might be the first time in her life she would do so, but it would not be the last.

In the library, she settled down on the edge of a blue velvet chair and began a light conversation with Matthew. Only half of her mind was on the discussion; the other half was reviewing the points she needed to emphasize in her meeting with Mr. McAllister.

My budget is small, the structural repairs are vital, I would like more light in the upper stories. The words ran through her head like lines of a memorized poem.

So intent was she on her preparation that she almost did not hear the butler announcing the arrival of Mr. Duncan McAllister. Willing herself to project assurance and calm, Emily stood to meet her visitor.

Almost immediately, she felt the urge to sit back down. Clarissa had told her that Mr. McAllister was competent, charming, and reasonable. Why had she neglected to mention that he was also striking?

The man in the doorway towered over Emily by a good eight inches. Granted, that was not difficult, seeing as she topped five feet by only an inch or two. But it was not his imposing height that first drew her attention. Rather, it was his shock of tousled russet hair, coupled with arresting hazel eyes, that distracted her.

Fortunately, she did not need to speak right away. Matthew had crossed the room to usher the visitor in. "Good afternoon, Mr. McAllister," he said, shaking his guest's hand. "Please let me introduce you to my sister-in-law, Lady Tuncliffe."

The architect strolled into the room with the easy grace of an athlete. He reminded Emily of a prime racehorse being forced to trot when he longed to canter.

"Good afternoon, my lady," he said in a pleasing, low voice as he bowed. She returned his greeting and curtseyed before he seated himself in a leather Queen Anne chair.

"I knew Lord Tuncliffe at Harrow. My condolences on his passing," Mr. McAllister continued. Despite his kind words, his voice had turned cool and impersonal when he spoke of her late husband.

Oh, good heavens, thought Emily. *Did every man across the length and breadth of England have a grudge against Simon?*

She would not be surprised. Simon was the sort of man who collected enemies the way other men collected rare coins.

The best way to deflect the conversation from Simon would be to start discussing the plans for her town house, Emily decided. "My sister and brother-in-law have spoken highly of you," she began. "I believe you have had a chance to inspect the property in Berkeley Square?"

Matthew, who had remained standing, moved toward the door. "I believe that is my cue to leave you to your business. But do call upon me if I can be of any assistance." He gave Emily an encouraging smile as he departed.

A light feather of panic tickled her stomach as she watched him go.

She willed herself to be calm and told herself that she could manage — even if this gentleman was not the middle-aged, balding personage she had for some reason envisioned.

"Yes, I visited your house this morning," Mr. McAllister said. She realized he was answering the question she had posed, and forced herself to concentrate. "You realize that you have your work cut out for you?"

"Indeed I do. My late husband left the house closed for many years, with no servants in residence."

Mr. McAllister nodded. "As a result, there is extensive water damage to the roof, and a great deal of dry rot along the west and north walls. The salon and two of the bedrooms, however, are habitable."

"I am glad to hear that, sir, as my funds are minuscule."

At this remark, the architect's eyes narrowed. "Minuscule? When I knew your late husband at Harrow, he had led us all to believe that his family was extremely wealthy."

Emily twisted her hands together. Was he accusing her of lying? What an inauspicious start to the negotiations.

But then she thought about his comment and realized he had every reason to be suspicious of her claim. Years ago, before Simon had begun drinking and gambling away every spare penny, the Tuncliffe estate had been a prosperous one, although by no means could it ever have been described as "extremely wealthy."

Simon had always had a tendency to exaggerate.

"The family fell on hard times in recent years," she said. "I am using the profits from the sale of a small, unentailed cottage in Kent to fund the restoration of the Berkeley Square property." Silently, she thanked heaven for the cottage, whose existence she had discovered only after Simon's death, when she had learned it and the town house had been willed to her.

The fact that Simon had died young was probably the only reason she had a roof over her head at all — if he had lived, it would only have been a matter of time before he would have gambled away both the cottage and the town house. Three years ago, he had lost his small hunting box in Melton Mowbray on a wager.

None of this did she want to share with Mr. McAllister, however. She felt guilty enough that she had not grieved her young husband's passing; she had no wish to compound her sins by denigrating Simon before a stranger.

Fortunately, the architect accepted her short but truthful explanation without comment.

"So what will be your total budget for this project?" he asked.

"I believe I can afford to pay six hundred pounds." Emily named a sum a little below her actual budget, as Matthew had advised her to do. She stilled her twisting hands with effort. Would the architect laugh in her face?

To her relief, he did not. He did, however, grimace. "It will be tight at that price, and no mistake, my lady," he said. For the first time, she caught the hint of a Scottish burr in his speech — just a slight roll to the "r" in "price."

"We need to discuss two things," he continued. "Some structural repairs will be necessary to make the house sound. They will not be particularly glamorous."

Emily nodded.

"The other changes will be more cosmetic: things such as paint, moldings, perhaps a new window or two."

Again, she nodded. "Let us begin with the structural changes, Mr. McAllister. We should make sure the house is of sound body before dressing it up in fine furs."

He raised his eyebrows. "That is a logical approach, Lady Tuncliffe."

"You seem surprised."

"Not surprised, exactly. It is just that most of my female clients seem more concerned with the flourishes and furbelows than the dull matters of repointing bricks and replacing floorboards."

"Most of your female clients, I assume, are working with their husbands to renovate their homes?"

"Yes."

"Well, you see, there is the difference. I must play the roles of both husband and wife." Emily was pleased with her response. It sounded firm and, well, independent.

16

She was further rewarded by a slow smile from Mr. McAllister. Until now, he had seemed every inch the sober, logical professional. The grin trimmed ten years from his face. She realized that he was likely not many years older than she.

"May I say that you are better suited to one role than the other one? Although with a good quality hat and a quizzing glass . . ." He tilted his head to one side, as if imagining her in mannish garb. "No, even with the right neckcloth, I doubt you would make a convincing husband."

She laughed. Clare had been right — Mr. McAllister was most personable. "Sadly, I must work within the constraints fate has given me."

"Well, then, I will just have to take your word that you are playing the gentleman's part at the moment. So let me tell you a bit about the wonders of plaster." They moved to chairs around a large oak table so that he could spread out his sketches.

Half an hour later, they had resolved numerous questions about the house's main structural problems. Emily had agreed to fix three leaky windows, a set of warped floorboards in the drawing room, much of the two dry-rotted walls, and a good portion of the roof, among other things. They had discussed alterations to the kitchen. She had also supported Mr. McAllister's suggestion to divide a large, dreary bedroom into two more serviceable rooms, and to expand the foyer to provide more room for guests to shed their wraps.

Emily was surprised at how straightforward the meeting had turned out to be. Mr. McAllister had considered her suggestions and answered her questions with patience.

Before they moved on to matters of paint and trimmings, however, she had one other major renovation to propose.

"Would it be feasible, Mr. McAllister, to enlarge the study at the back of the house by demolishing this wall, here?" She pointed to a spot on his rough sketch of the ground floor.

He examined the drawing, tapping his finger against the surface of the mahogany library table. "I suppose so," he conceded. "I do not believe that is a load-bearing wall. But there are already several larger rooms in the house. Would the considerable expense needed to enlarge this one be justified?"

Emily hesitated. How could she explain that the study was the only room in the house with the proper lighting to serve as a studio, without provoking a long discussion of her hobby?

"I like this room's view of the garden," she replied. Well, it was the truth. It just was not the whole truth.

He pulled a sheet of paper toward him and made some sketches and calculations. She watched with interest, scarcely daring to hope that her dream of a studio would be possible.

"I would need to take some measurements and to examine that wall more thoroughly," he said. "But I believe the cost to expand the study would be approximately one hundred and fifty pounds."

"One hundred and fifty pounds?" Emily sagged back against her chair, sick with disappointment. Such a sum was beyond her budget — not far beyond, but she was determined not to give in to wild flights of fancy.

If she was to be a widow of independent means, she had to be careful with her limited funds.

"Lady Tuncliffe?" Mr. McAllister's voice broke into her thoughts. "I am sorry about the expense, but I assure you that it is a fairly accurate estimate. I realize that you may not be able to take on this project and do all the structural repairs, as well."

"No, I appreciate your honesty, Mr. McAllister." Emily dismissed her daydream with a quick wave of her hand. Perhaps in the future, somehow, she would build her studio. She must be content, for now, with simply having a home of her own.

"Let us forget the study for now. If I leave it alone, I will have a little money left over to paint the three habitable rooms, will I not?"

"Certainly," Mr. McAllister replied, giving her a shrewd glance. She had the uneasy suspicion he knew how much she had set her heart on that studio.

They discussed paint shades and the cost to replace a cracked molding in one of the bedrooms. Within twenty minutes they were done, and Emily was sorry. It had been an enjoyable conversation.

"Thank you for your efforts, Mr. McAllister," she said as she stood up from the table.

"Thank you for considering me, Lady Tuncliffe," he replied, rising as well. "It has been a pleasure doing business with both your gentlemanly and distaff sides."

She smiled at his gentle teasing.

"Take some time to think about my estimate," he added. "Talk it over with Lord and Lady Langdon. If you decide to use my services, please let me know."

He walked around to her side of the table, and once again she noted his fluid grace. With his lithe frame and easy humor, he was about as different from her pudgy, irritable husband as it was possible for a man to be.

Perhaps, if she decided to hire him, they might in time become friends. It would be nice to meet some new people in London.

Emily was by nature shy, and the few intimates she had had during her London childhood had scattered to the four corners of England. None of them had been gentlemen, she acknowledged, but with Mr. McAllister she had quickly developed a camaraderie that she had rarely felt with anyone of either sex.

She was looking forward to this renovation project very much indeed, she thought, as she walked him to the door.

Two

"Good afternoon, Penny," Duncan McAllister said, entering his small sitting room and stooping to kiss his sister on the cheek. "I'm surprised to see you indoors on such a fine afternoon."

Penelope McAllister put down her needlework and smiled. She had her brother's ruddy coloring and hazel eyes, but not his height. He had only recently stopped calling her *scradyn,* at her laughing insistence. At three and twenty, she had protested, she was far too old for childhood nicknames — especially one meaning "runt."

Her smile cheered him. As he often did, Duncan offered up a silent word of thanks to the powers that be that Penny had come south to keep his house and keep him company after Olivia died. Without his sister, he would have come apart utterly in those first dreadful months.

"I am indoors at the moment because I promised Susannah I would take her to the park later," his sister replied. "She is asleep now — after a protracted struggle.

I do not envy Nurse!"

Duncan grinned. His three-year-old daughter resisted naptime with the same ferocity a notorious rake would use to resist domestication.

"Well, since you are here, I would like to discuss a possible commission with you. I always value your counsel, and this is a rather perplexing situation."

Penny nodded. "Certainly. I hope I can help."

Duncan settled down at his desk, attempting to clear a space in the clutter of papers, bills, invitations, and correspondence that obscured the rosewood surface. Deciding that was a fruitless task, he laid the notes he had made during his meeting with Lady Tuncliffe on top of everything else.

"Honestly, Duncan, I cannot understand how you can be so meticulous about virtually everything and yet have a desk that looks as though it has been through a windstorm," Penny said with mock exasperation.

"It is like a magnet that attracts all my disorder, so I can keep the rest of my life pristine. I find it an admirable system. Perhaps I could write a monograph on the subject."

"I'm sorry, I should not bait you," Penny said, little evidence of contrition in her voice. "But let us move on to more important matters. What is this new commission?"

"It is an opportunity to renovate a rather dilapidated town house on Berkeley Square — if the client likes my recommendations and estimate."

"Berkeley Square!" His sister's eyes widened. "That is one of the most prestigious areas of Mayfair! It would be a wonderful chance to demonstrate your skills to some of the *ton*'s richest families. Why are you hesitating?"

"For the most ridiculous of reasons, I know. And yet, it troubles me." Duncan leaned forward in his chair, resting his elbows on his knees. "I have just returned from meeting the client, a woman named Lady Tuncliffe."

"Why does that name sound so familiar?"

"Perhaps because, long ago, you may have heard me complain about a classmate of mine at Harrow named Simon Wallace. He later came into the title of Viscount Tuncliffe, and the Lady Tuncliffe in question is his widow."

"I do remember you mentioning

Simon," Penny said. "Was he the one who was so cruel to the younger boys, and who mocked your accent?"

"Yes, it was he." The short reply conveyed none of the lingering animosity Duncan felt toward the callous schoolboy who had made his life such a misery during his early years at Harrow. Not only had Simon ridiculed his accent, he had jeered Duncan's origins — "the son of a mere merchant" had been the kindest of his gibes.

"But your accent should not cause you any worry now," Penny said. "I never noticed it, of course, but others seem to be surprised to learn that you are a Scot, despite your name."

Sadly, that was true. Stung by Wallace's words, Duncan had worked diligently to suppress every "aye" and "nae." Now, his native dialect only surfaced when he was emotional or tired, or in the company of family.

"It is not good for a man to be ashamed of his origins," Duncan replied.

"If you ever returned to Edinburgh, you would regain your accent in no time."

"Perhaps." He had no plans to return to Scotland in the foreseeable future, at least until his architectural practice was flourishing once more.

Returning his thoughts to his nemesis at Harrow, Duncan reflected that Simon Wallace had done him one inadvertent favor. Due to the other boy's teasing, Duncan had resolved to win friends just to spite him. He had joined every sporting team at school and soon excelled in everything from fencing to cricket. This early involvement in sport had given him a lifelong network of friends and an interest in physical pursuits, both of which had stood him in good stead over the years.

That didn't mean he resented Simon Wallace any less, however.

"So you are concerned that Lady Tuncliffe may be cut from the same cloth as your schoolmate?" Penny asked, moving to the heart of the matter as usual.

"Yes. I cannot imagine that anyone could be married to such a man without possessing, or acquiring, a demanding nature. I am concerned she may be deceitful, as well. Wallace always boasted of the extent of his fortune, and yet she tells me her budget for the renovation is modest."

"It would be simple, would it not, for a determined young man to dissipate a family fortune if he were so inclined?"

"You are right, it would. And if there was

ever a boy destined to grow into a libertine, it was Simon Wallace. Fortunately, our paths never crossed after we left Harrow, although I did know that he had died several years ago. Read it in the *Times*. It was a riding accident."

"In your meeting with Lady Tuncliffe, did you perceive any unpleasant characteristics in her?"

As Duncan recalled the meeting, the first memory that flooded his brain was anything but unpleasant. He remembered, of all things, the light violet perfume that she wore.

"Quite the contrary," he replied. "She was charming and, I believe, rather shy. I suspect that it was the first time in her life that she had engaged in a business negotiation. She appeared to be making a conscious effort to overcome her nervousness."

"She certainly does not sound like an ogre. If she wants to hire you — and who would not! — I think you should take on this commission wholeheartedly. At the very least, you will have the satisfaction of repairing a house that the odious Lord Tuncliffe sorely neglected."

"The house needs a great deal of work," Duncan said, picking up his notes and scanning them. "But it has marvelous potential! The moldings in the salon need just a touch of paint and plaster to regain their former elegance, and Lady Tuncliffe has agreed that it would be wise to remodel one ghastly bedroom into two smaller rooms. I was thinking one would make a cozy library, with floor-to-ceiling oak shelves. And I could extend the existing windows down to the floor to allow more light."

Penny laughed. "I have not seen you this excited about a project in a long time."

"Perhaps because I have so few projects these days to excite me. If no new ones materialize, I may soon find myself a gentleman of leisure. Perhaps I shall take up gambling as my new career. Or excessive drinking — I have heard that has its charms." He stroked his chin in mock thought.

"Do not torture yourself. You do good work, and your clients refer you to others. These last few months are just a brief anomaly."

"Clients refer me to others, but then the commission falls through before the papers are signed. I cannot understand it. People seem to like my proposals, then they withdraw at the last minute." He glanced up at his sister and lowered his voice to a theatrical whisper. "Do you suppose they have heard of the bodies I have buried in the cellar?"

"You are incorrigible! Perhaps they are crying off because they perceive your lack of proper adult seriousness."

"Whatever the reason, I very much hope that Lady Tuncliffe does not follow this pattern."

"She will be a fool if she does."

Duncan smiled, warmed by his sister's boundless confidence in him. Perhaps she was right, and his luck was turning at last.

"Thank you, Penny. As usual, your counsel has been wise."

She stood and sketched a mock little bow. "Your humble servant, sir."

He glanced at the clock. "How long, do you suppose, will Susannah be asleep?"

"At least another hour, I would imagine."

"Well, then, I think I shall repair to Gentleman Jackson's rooms for a round or two." Duncan rose from his chair.

"I must admit, the distinction between pugilism and ordinary fisticuffs is lost on me. Did not Father punish you and Neil for the same activities that you now classify as sport?"

Duncan grinned. "Well, we were not nearly as adept as the boxers at Jackson's — even if we made up in boyish enthusiasm what we lacked in skill. Fortunately, we never meant to hurt each other." He crossed to the door. "I will be back in a few hours. Enjoy your jaunt to the park."

As Emily examined some rough drawings of the town house that Mr. McAllister had left for her perusal, she laughed in sheer, untrammeled joy. Aside from her disappointment about the studio, she was pleased with the plans. She would be mistress of her own house at last.

"What is so amusing?" Clarissa asked, entering the room.

"Nothing, really. I am just excited about Mr. McAllister's ideas. Look!" She slid the sketches across the library table to her sister.

"Very nice," Clarissa pronounced after leafing through them. She passed them back to Emily and sat down at one end of an L-shaped sofa close to the fireplace. The spring day was mild, but the sunshine had not entirely penetrated the cool library. "So you have decided to retain his services?"

"Oh, I think I will. Your recommendation alone was enough to convince me, and now that I have met him, I know we will work well together." Emily smiled, recalling Mr. McAllister's smooth voice with just a trace of Scottish lilt. That alone would make their meetings pleasant.

"Did he indicate how long the work might take?"

"Perhaps two months to do everything. But three rooms need only a cleaning and a light coat of paint. I could move in next week!"

"Before month's end!" Clarissa's voice was aghast. "It will be chaos, amid all the dust and workers and noise."

"But the salon and two bedrooms are almost completely undamaged. I would need to keep most of my clothing and precious things in storage, of course, but I could begin setting up my household. And, if I were on the premises, I could supervise the proceedings much more easily." Emily, feeling rather stiff after sitting so long on one of the hard mahogany chairs surrounding the table, moved to sit on the other half of Clarissa's sofa.

"Perhaps, but it still seems rather imprudent."

"This from a girl who thought nothing of running off to the Canadas, not so long ago. I believe marriage has made you conventional, Clare."

"Don't insult me!" her sister cried. "You will never let me live that down, will you?"

Before their marriage, Clarissa and Matthew had had a rancorous disagreement, and Clarissa had boldly decided to accept a post as a governess in the wilds somewhere north of the United States. Only a hasty intervention by Matthew had scuttled the plan.

"But seriously, Em, you should not feel that your only choice is to move to Berkeley Square. I would love your company at Langdon Hall." Clarissa was due to leave shortly for Oxfordshire, to visit relatives before she became too *enceinte* to travel comfortably. "I will be lonely without Matthew, but he has to stay in Town because Parliament is in session."

At this juncture, Lord Langdon strolled into the room. "Problems?" he asked, raising his bushy black brows.

"Not in the least," Emily said. "I was just explaining to Clare that several rooms in the town house will soon be habitable, and that it makes sense for me to move into them as soon as possible."

"A wise decision," Matthew said, folding his considerable height into the Queen

Anne chair. "That way, you will be available to deal with any problems that arise."

Emily shot her younger sister a triumphant glance.

"Well, you are little help," Clarissa told her husband.

"I am a politician — I examine the facts and then vote with my conscience. And I'm afraid I must agree with Emily on this one."

"Thank you, Matthew. It is gratifying to have a male agree with me for a change."

"You must promise me one thing, though. If the noise and confusion become overwhelming, you must feel free to retreat here to Stonecourt, even in Clarissa's absence." Matthew sighed. "It is a shame Uncle Walter is no longer here. The two of you would have been excellent company for each other." Matthew's uncle, who had raised him after the death of his parents, had passed away the previous year.

"That would have been lovely," Emily said. She had been fond of the elderly gentleman. "And I do thank you for your kind offer. I will certainly take advantage of it if the need arises. But somehow, I think that the town house would have to be falling down about my ears before I would concede to leave it."

Three

As she scrubbed a persistent smear on one of the salon's large windows, Emily wondered how long it had been since anyone had washed anything in the Berkeley Square house.

She paused in her work to glance around the airy room with satisfaction. Mr. McAllister had been right; several coats of pale yellow paint had done wonders to brighten up the salon. Once she had moved in her few bits of furniture, it would be a charming room.

There would be enough time for daydreaming later, she told herself. Diligently, she reapplied herself to the window, singing an old folk song as she worked. Within a few minutes, it had begun to gleam like an Oxford Street display case.

"Lady Tuncliffe! You shouldn't be doing that!" Gertie's voice echoed behind her.

Emily turned from her work and smiled at the middle-aged, dark-haired housemaid. Gertie, who had been with her since the beginning of Emily's marriage to Simon, had always been as fiercely protective of her as a mother cat.

"It is a job that needs to be done, and if you are to do everything in this house, you will be exhausted and leave me within weeks," Emily replied. "Besides, I enjoy it."

It was true. Household tasks that normally would have bored her had taken on new meaning since she had opened the house in Berkeley Square. Every job completed brought her one step closer to the vision in her mind's eye.

Gertie gave her an indulgent look. "You're an odd duck, and that's for certain. Enjoying washing windows! Well, I shan't argue too long with you, m'lady. If it makes you happy, then by all means do it. Just mind you don't ruin your lovely hands. Wear one of your old pairs of gloves. I'll be in what passes for a kitchen in this house — ring for me if you need help."

"I will, Gertie, thanks," she called out as the little housemaid departed. Emily was just about to go upstairs to search for a pair of gloves when there was a knock at the front door.

"I will answer it, Gertie," she called out, tugging down the sleeves of her ancient day dress as she hurried out of the salon and along the corridor. She wondered who on earth it could be. Few people knew she was in residence.

As she swept a few stray locks of hair back from her face, she hoped her caller was not Mr. McAllister. She would hate to encounter him in such a disheveled state, even though he was just her architect and she was just his client.

Emily went down the stairs, crossed the small foyer, and opened the front door, which squeaked on its hinges. A familiar figure stood grinning on the step.

"Alex!" she cried, hurtling into his arms for a hug. "We were not expecting you back in Town for at least a week!"

Alexander Denham, Viscount Rossley, was as tall and dark as his eldest sister was small and fair. At six feet, he towered over everyone in the family — much to the chagrin of their father, who found he could no longer cow his only son quite as effectively as he had been able to do just a few years ago.

"I thought I would surprise you all," he replied, squeezing her. "Lud, it is good to see you, Em — even if you do look as though you have been in a street fight. What on earth have you been doing?"

"Cleaning," she replied, leading him past

the dilapidated rooms on the ground floor and upstairs. When they reached the salon, she frowned. "I am afraid there are few places to sit, but I do have one good piece of furniture," she said, ushering him to a chaise longue upholstered in worn green silk, which she had found in the house when she moved in.

"Why have you been cleaning? Should you not be letting the servants do that?"

"You are as bad as Gertie." Emily laughed. "I have only one servant at the moment, two perfectly capable hands, and an entire house that needs work. You are lucky you arrived late in the day, or the place would have been alive with carpenters."

"I stopped by Clare's first, but she was just about to leave for Langdon Hall. She told me you had moved in here already, but I did not realize that the house was not finished!"

"It will be, soon enough. Would you like something to eat?"

"You know me too well, Em. As usual, I am famished."

Within minutes, Gertie had worked her usual magic and conjured up a light meal of bread, cold meat, and cheese. The siblings ate sitting side by side on the chaise in the salon, since the dining room was still unusable.

"So what brought you to London early?"

Her brother wiped his mouth with a linen napkin. "I am trying to get some small advantage over my fellow graduates. Seems everyone is coming to Town, and rooms are scarce, especially for one such as I whose pockets are somewhat to let. I hope to contact several acquaintances to enquire whether they are seeking to share their lodgings."

"You should live here!" Emily said. "That is, if you can bear the dust and the noise."

"Oh, Em, I would not mind that in the slightest, but I doubt you want me hanging about. I know how much you have wanted a home of your own. Clare told me."

"I hope she did not think me rude to decline her hospitality," Emily said, rising to pour herself and Alex two cups of tea from the chipped Wedgwood pot balanced precariously on the mantelpiece.

"Not at all. She understood."

"Well, having a houseguest does not make me any less independent. In fact, I may even put you to work." Emily knew that Alex would not agree if there was any hint of charity in the proposal.

"I would be more than happy to earn my keep," he replied, confirming her suspicions. "But I may be coming and going at odd hours."

"You are just down from Oxford, and entitled to some fun. I promise not to say one word — to you, or to Papa." She turned from the mantel and smiled. "However, if you do not wish to live here, you could always take up residence with him."

At this idea, both siblings laughed. "We would be at daggers drawn within the week, and well you know it," Alex said. "I respect him as my father, but that does not mean I can live with him again."

"I feel quite the same way," Emily said. She had never wholly forgiven her father for browbeating her into marrying Simon Wallace, even though she had acquiesced and done what she had believed to be her duty.

They lapsed into a companionable silence as they sipped their tea.

"So, will you be my first houseguest?" Emily asked. "I would dearly love to be able to finally show some hospitality. Simon was so . . . well, he was never . . ."

"I know, Em." Alex reached over and awkwardly patted his sister's hand. "Clare told me how much he complained when she came to stay, years ago. You are well rid of him."

"Do not speak so!"

"It is the truth."

"Even if it were, it would be disloyal to say so." Emily paused, trying to marshal her thoughts. "You and Clarissa are the only ones who understand what my life was like in Hampshire. But if I had just been a better wife, perhaps he would have been happier."

"You are too critical of yourself. Do not give Simon the satisfaction of haunting you!"

To her chagrin, Emily felt a thin mist film her eyes. She swallowed with difficulty. "Thank you, Alex. You have always been one of my most stalwart defenders, and I do appreciate it."

During her marriage, there had been days when she had been certain all her miseries were of her own making. Only her siblings' assurances had helped her cope. Even Lucy, her youngest sister, had written sweet, loving letters that had helped on the worst days.

But that part of her life was over.

"Let us not waste any more time speaking of Simon," she said, passing her brother a plate of small cakes from the local confectioner's. "Are you prepared to camp here like a footloose soldier? I can offer you a freshly painted room and an adequate bed, but everything else is rather rustic, I am afraid."

"Em, I have just come from three years of student lodgings. It will be a palace in comparison — particularly as I will have no need to share it with Papa!" He grinned as he helped himself to two morsels of cake. "We should invite Lucy over frequently as well. It seems unfair that she should be the only one left to cope with his moods."

"That's an excellent idea. Although this may be her last year at Denham House, as well. She is absolutely over the moon about making her debut. If my renovations progress as quickly as I hope, I will host a small party here for her during her season."

"We will all play together as we did when we were children!" Alex cried. "Clare and Matthew are welcome to come, as well, as long as they agree not to behave like old married people."

"It is settled, then. Shall I show you to your room, my lord?"

"By all means, Lady Tuncliffe. And thank you."

"Do not thank me yet until you have spent a day or two here with the builders," Emily replied with a laugh as she led her brother upstairs.

A few days later, when Alex was meeting a friend in St. James's, Emily was unpacking some small items from a crate in the salon. Mr. McAllister had covered all the doors leading into the salon with double layers of sheeting, which along with the doors themselves kept out most of the dirt and plaster dust. As a result, Emily felt confident about displaying some of her few treasures.

She smiled as she unwrapped a cloisonné figurine that a friend had given her shortly before her marriage. It had always reminded her of happier times. As she set it down on the mantelpiece, she thought it might be a good talisman for her new home.

Already, she felt more at home in Berkeley Square than she had ever felt at Simon's country estate. The Hampshire home had been drafty and isolated, and the servants had treated her with distant deference. Simon had resisted her few suggestions for improvements, even though most of the décor and furnishings dated from his grandfather's time. It had been rather like living in a neglected museum.

Above her head, she heard a clunk and a muttered exclamation. Mr. McAllister or one of the carpenters must have dropped a hammer.

Life as a London widow certainly differed from life as a sheltered single woman or a rusticating country wife, Emily thought as she withdrew another carefully wrapped item from the crate. When she had been young, the very thought of her being alone in the house with a man — let alone with several — with no one but a servant for company would have sent Emily's mother into fits. And at Tuncliffe Manor, people visited so seldom that the issue never arose. It felt odd to hear so many other people moving about the house — odd, but not troubling.

At the sound of footsteps on the stair, she raised her head. She had quickly learned to differentiate Mr. McAllister's step from those of his workers. He had a habit of joining her for a cup of tea and some biscuits in the afternoon. Sometimes they discussed her opinions on topics such as window sashes and floor finishes. But often they simply chatted, having discovered many mutual interests.

He popped his head through the curtain

shrouding the door. "Good afternoon, Lady Tuncliffe. Do you mind if I join you?"

With his hair tousled and flecked with dust, he looked a bit like a mischievous boy — but only a bit. No child commanded a room the way Mr. McAllister did, simply by entering it. Perhaps his air of authority was due to the years he had spent supervising the activities of carpenters and apprentices.

"I would enjoy the company, Mr. McAllister. Shall I ring for tea?" She already knew the answer, but formality dictated that she ask anyway. She moved to the chaise longue and sat down.

"Yes, thank you," he replied, stepping through the drapery.

The smile that had sprung to her lips when he first addressed her faded when he walked into the room. In his hand he carried a small oil painting of a maid hanging laundry out to dry.

She rang the bell for tea, hoping the sound might distract him from the question she feared he would ask.

"This is delightful," he said, holding the picture up. "I have learned a great deal over the years about painting, but I do not recognize this artist's work. Is he English?"

Flustered, Emily looked down into her lap. Perhaps she could lie.

She dismissed that idea. Not only was she a terrible liar, she had no wish to be deceitful — especially to Mr. McAllister.

To give herself time to think, she asked, "Where did you find that?"

Of course, she knew where he had found it, and she could have kicked herself for leaving it in plain view. Most of her artworks were in storage at Clarissa's house, but she had put two of her favorites in one of the disused bedrooms upstairs. She had hoped to hang them in her own bedroom, once she had finished arranging the furniture to her liking.

"I found it in the west bedroom," he said. "I hope you do not mind that I moved it. I needed to check the wall behind it for dry rot."

"Yes, of course. No, I do not mind." How was she going to explain this?

"So who is the artist? He has an intriguing style."

"It is not a he, in fact. It is a she." She sighed, giving up any hope of pretence. "I am the artist."

"You?" Surprise laced his voice. "But why are you so reluctant to admit it? This painting and its companion upstairs are both lovely."

"Thank you. I am glad you like them." Emily's voice was stiff. So few people had ever seen her paintings that she was unused to discussing them.

"I am surprised you have not hung them here in the salon. They are far superior, in my estimation, to that landscape on the far wall, which makes me long for a warm coat every time I look on it."

Emily glanced at the dull image of a ruined castle next to a lonely lake. The picture did not appeal to her, either, but it had been in the house when she arrived and she had decided that hanging it was better than living with empty walls. "You are far too kind. I create my paintings for my own amusement, but I am no artist."

"If you are no artist, then I am no architect. And if that is the case, I have a number of former clients who deserve an explanation." As he settled down on a chair Emily had recently resurrected from the cellar, Gertie entered with the tea.

"Oh, you've taken my advice and decided to hang that down here where everyone can see it!" the maid exclaimed as she set the tray down on a scuffed but still serviceable Sheraton table that Emily had borrowed from her mother. "It is such a pretty picture. Agnes never looked as good as she does right there!"

"I have not decided to hang it in the salon," Emily said, picking up the teapot. "That will be all, Gertie."

Gertie, apparently having the good sense to recognize one of her mistress's rare stubborn moods, withdrew.

"You prefer your tea clear, Mr. McAllister, do you not?"

"Yes, same as always," he replied in a distracted voice. He was still examining the painting. "The element that charms me so about this painting is the lightness of it. I can almost feel the wind blowing through the shirt in the maid's hands."

"Yes, but it is not a fit subject for art," Emily muttered.

"Why not? Because it does not depict some rich man's wife, covered in jewels, with a bad-tempered pug at her side?"

"For many reasons. It is a commonplace scene, done in commonplace colors. And it is much too bold," Emily said, repeating all the things that Simon had told her. "And it is not proper for a woman to work in oils. I should have been satisfied with water-colors."

"Why were you dissatisfied with them?"

"They were too tepid. I could not capture scenes the way I saw them. The way I felt them." She spooned some sugar into her tea and stirred it.

"Then you were right to use oils. Why settle for something lackluster when better materials are available? It is like using soft pine for one's floors when you can afford marble."

"That is how I have always felt, although, heaven knows, there were times when the expense of oils felt decadent." In painful detail, Emily remembered the early morning when Simon had found some painting supplies she had hidden in an old trunk. He might not have reacted so precipitately, had he not just come home from a long night of drinking at a neighbor's house.

"You take the money I give you to buy food and waste it on nonsense like paint?" he had bellowed, holding up a palette as though it were a piece of rotten meat. "Paint for your foolish daubings of housemaids and dogs?"

"I have not used the household money for paint," Emily had protested. "I used some of the money my grandmother gave me."

"Stop lying to me!" Simon had roared,

picking up the palette and opening the window. "All you do is nag and lie, nag and lie . . ."

"I do not! I have not!"

Her protests had been to no avail. Simon had tossed every palette and brush in the trunk out the window, before lurching off to bed. It had taken her the better part of the morning to retrieve them from the garden. After that, she had hidden them in the cellar.

"Lady Tuncliffe?" Mr. McAllister's warm baritone brought her back to the present.

"Please forgive me. I was woolgathering. What did you say?"

"I just said that you have a wonderful eye for detail." He sipped his tea. "Do you have many other pieces?"

"About twenty or so. Most of them are in storage at my sister's house, until the renovations here are complete. But this one and the other upstairs are two of my favorites. I am planning to hang them in my bedroom."

"I agree with Gertie. You should hang them down here, where all may enjoy them."

"Few find scenes of washerwomen and gardeners uplifting." Emily shifted in her chair and looked about the room. She noticed a small chip in the wainscoting, and seized on it. "I have been meaning to mention some additional repairs in this room."

But Mr. McAllister did not hear her. "You must enjoy such scenes, or else you would not paint them."

"Many do not, or one would see them hanging in galleries, alongside artworks of men in battle and gods at play." She lifted the teapot. "Would you like another cup?"

"Why should you care what artworks others like? This is your house."

Emily sighed. Mr. McAllister had the tenacity of a young debutante seeking an introduction to the latest pink of the *ton*. "Yes, but if I hang the paintings down here, others will ask — as you have — where they came from."

"Why would that be a problem?"

Emily set down the teapot and twisted her hands. Why could he not understand?

"Because I am a lady, and a lady should only paint cheerful watercolor landscapes, if anything."

"Is there a law to that effect? Perhaps, then, we should petition your brother-in-law to introduce a new bill in the House of Lords: 'An Act Respecting the Freedom of Females to Use the Full Range of Artistic

50

Materials.' I am surprised the idea has not occurred to him already. He seems a right-thinking man."

"Be serious." Despite her discomfort with the whole subject, Emily smiled.

"I am. Who says you must use water-colors?"

"I say. Everyone says."

"I do not say. I think your work is charming, and that you should not care what others think." Mr. McAllister's voice had lost its teasing tone. He had set down his teacup and was staring at her with alarming intensity. His hazel eyes seemed almost emerald in the late afternoon light.

It would be unnerving to be subject to such a glance often.

"It is simple for you to say that the opinions of others are of no consequence." A bitter undertone laced her words.

"Because I am a man?"

Emily nodded.

"Your sister does not care what others think. I realized that about two hours after we started to work together. Do you realize it was her idea to paint the conservatory walls deep red?"

Emily laughed. "Yes, that is Clare's way. She is the rebellious one in the family, while I am the conventional one."

"Her idea worked, though. The walls warm up the room marvelously. Otherwise, it could have been quite stark, with that one north-facing window."

As Mr. McAllister bit into a biscuit, his eyes widened. Quickly, he swallowed. "Now I know why you wanted to open up that south-facing room at the back of this house. You wanted it for a studio!"

Emily could think of no way to deny it. "I realize it was a fanciful idea."

"It was an excellent idea — it is the best room in the house for such a use. You must expand it in the future, if you are financially able."

"Perhaps. More tea?"

"You have an admirable gift for deflecting a conversation." He chuckled. "But seriously, Lady Tuncliffe, you also have artistic talent. Do not hide your light under a bushel."

"You are too kind," she said again. Heat flooded her cheeks. Few people had ever seen her paintings, and fewer still had liked them. Even though she suspected that Mr. McAllister was simply being polite, she reveled in his appreciation of her work.

But no matter what he said, she would not hang the paintings in the salon. Painting in oils was an occupation for bohemian artists, not gently reared widows. Simon's outrageous antics during his short life had already made her somewhat suspect among the more proper members of the *ton*. She would not give them another reason to cut her.

If she was to live as a widow of independent means, above all she must be respectable.

"I appreciate your thoughts on my work, but I would truly prefer to speak of other matters, Mr. McAllister," she said with a firmness that surprised her. "I had some thoughts on the hardware for the dining room door, which you asked me about yesterday."

To her relief, the architect took her hint and let the subject of the paintings drop. When he had finished his tea, however, he tried a different tack.

"Perhaps you should hang just one of your paintings here, on a trial basis. If the streets of Mayfair erupt in outraged protest, you could simply remove the offending article." A huge grin split the planes of his face as he stood.

The man should have been an actor, Emily thought. There would be many female theatergoers who would find his visage — as well as the rest of him —

reason alone to attend a performance.

It was astonishing that he was unmarried.

Emily set down her cup with such force that it rattled in its saucer. Where had that thought come from?

She realized that she did not know for certain that he was unmarried. Details of their childhoods they had shared, and views on architecture and music and gardens. But she had avoided bringing up the topic of marriage and children for fear of encouraging Mr. McAllister to ask her questions about her own experience in those areas. Since he had never mentioned a wife or children — but had, several times, mentioned his sister Penny, who lived with him — she had assumed he was a bachelor.

Whether he was or not was no concern of hers.

Mr. McAllister was looking at her curiously. She realized she had not responded to his sally about riots in the streets.

"I would hate to be the cause of civic unrest, Mr. McAllister," she said with a light laugh, standing up to see him out. "No, in the interests of the public peace, I think the paintings will remain my secret."

He gave a gusty sigh, and once again she

reflected that he could have had a successful career on the stage. "As you wish, my lady. I am just the hired help."

"No, Mr. McAllister, you are my friend, and I value your opinion." Worried that she had offended him, she extended her hand. "Please accept my apologies for my rudeness."

With a quizzical look, he accepted her outstretched hand and squeezed it gently. A quiver ran across her skin from her fingers to the soles of her feet as he clasped her hand in his larger one.

"No apologies needed," he said, his voice low. "Friends must always feel free to speak frankly."

With that, he gave a polite bow. "Thank you for the tea." He slipped through the sheets draped across the doorway.

Rattled, Emily sat back down on the chaise longue, her unpacking forgotten for the moment. Never had a man's touch resonated through her so strongly. What would it be like to feel his hand on her elbow during a country dance, or at her waist during the now acceptable waltz?

She shook her head. Such thoughts were inappropriate for a sober widow — particularly one who fully intended to remain that way. Her experience with marriage had given her little inclination to enter the institution of holy matrimony a second time.

And even were she so inclined, she was unfit to be any man's wife.

Pushing her idle speculations about Mr. McAllister from her head, she strode across the room and knelt down next to the packing crate once more.

Four

Duncan sharpened the nib of his pen, dipped it in his silver inkwell, and added up the column of figures for the third time. For the third time, he got the same unappealing total.

If business did not improve in the next few months, he would have to take drastic action. He could not continue to run this small house, and to support Penny and Susannah, if he could not secure more work.

He could not understand the downturn in his business. Other architects said that they were busier than ever this year. Duncan had accepted several prestigious commissions the previous autumn. But this spring, if not for Lady Tuncliffe's renovation and a few smaller projects, he would be unemployed.

The thought of Lady Tuncliffe brought a smile to his face. He was astonished that he had ever suspected her of possessing a personality similar to her late husband's. She had been unfailingly demure and gracious to him during their acquaintance —

even during the discussion of her paintings, when he had sensed a deep stubborn streak in her that could have led to a much more acrimonious discussion.

But there were stronger emotions running through her than mere stubbornness. He thought back to the moment when they had clasped hands the other day. In her blue-eyed gaze, he had detected a glimmer of something that was not at all demure.

And in response, he had felt a tremor of interest such as he had not felt since Olivia had died. Perhaps it was time to think about remarrying.

True, he was unlikely to find another wife whom he would love as he had loved Olivia. But Lady Tuncliffe seemed agreeable, and he enjoyed spending time with her. And it would be good for Susannah to have a stepmother.

What was wrong with him? He tossed the pen down on his disordered desk in disgust. Even if he had been interested in courting a woman, he was in no position even to think about such a thing at the moment. A man with a failing business was not exactly the prize of the marriage market. In addition, Lady Tuncliffe was a somewhat recent widow. It could be inappropriate to begin a courtship with her so soon.

A knock at the door interrupted his musings. He heard Libby, their maid of all work, answer the summons.

"Mr. McAllister?" She came into the room a moment later. "Lord Rossley is here to see you."

Rossley? Duncan was momentarily puzzled, until he remembered that Rossley was Lady Tuncliffe's brother. She had mentioned that he was staying with her for a few months, but Duncan had not met him yet. "Please show him in, Libby."

He rose from his desk as the dark-haired man entered. Lord Rossley was as tall as he, but considerably less solid; he had still to grow into his substantial frame. Lady Tuncliffe had said her brother was just down from Oxford, so he must not be far past one and twenty.

"Good afternoon, my lord," Duncan said, extending his hand. "I am pleased to make your acquaintance."

"The pleasure is mine." The other man shook with a firm grip. "My sister has spoken highly of you."

"The admiration is mutual. She is both a charming lady and a perspicacious client." He motioned Lord Rossley into the room. "Please sit down. May I offer you some refreshments?"

The younger man's eyes lit up. "That would be kind, sir. I have been running about town all day."

Duncan rang for Libby and asked her to fetch Penny, as well as a tea tray.

"I have come to deliver this for my sister," said Lord Rossley, reaching into the pocket of his well-tailored coat and withdrawing a small bundle of bank notes wrapped in a sheet of paper. "It should cover the balance of the fee for your work to date. We felt it was too valuable to entrust to a messenger."

Duncan accepted the bundle and placed it on his desk. Realizing that it might easily be lost amid the piles of papers, he retrieved it and put it in a small drawer. "Thank you. I appreciate your prompt payment."

He turned as Penny entered the room. "May I introduce you to my sister, Penelope McAllister? Penny, this is Lord Rossley, the brother of my client, Lady Tuncliffe."

Penny, to his astonishment, began to blush right to the roots of her ginger hair. He could not recall seeing her turn pink since she had been a young girl in the schoolroom.

"Welcome to our home, Lord Rossley,"

she said with a brief curtsey.

"I am pleased to make your acquaintance," Rossley replied in a voice that had suddenly risen half an octave.

At that moment, Libby arrived with the tea tray. Penny hurried to her customary seat on the sofa and began to pour.

"So, do you live in London, my lord?" she asked.

"I have just recently returned, after reading classics at Oxford," he replied.

"Classics! How interesting!"

"Not terribly, as a matter of fact," Lord Rossley replied with a rueful grin. "My sister, Clarissa, is the intellectual bright light in our family, not I."

"So what will you do, now that you have finished?" Penny handed their guest a cup of tea.

"Try to stay out of trouble for the Season, I suppose. After that, I will go to our estate in Kent to begin my training in estate management, as I will inherit my father's title one day. But enough about me. I can tell from your voice that you are not a native Londoner."

Duncan watched with growing amusement as the two younger people chatted. It was clear that they had largely forgotten his presence.

Just as he was reaching for a ginger biscuit, he heard a commotion outside the door. Moments later, a small whirlwind burst in.

"Biscuits!" exclaimed Susannah, her wide blue eyes riveted on the tea tray. Then, suddenly aware of the stranger in the room, she popped a finger into her mouth and hung her head shyly. Her eyes, however, remained trained on the plate of sweets.

"I'm sorry, Mr. McAllister," said Nurse from the doorway. "She was insistent on seeing you, but I didn't realize you had a visitor."

"Please, do not remove this charming young lady on my account," said Lord Rossley, crossing the room and crouching down in front of the child. "Good afternoon," he said gravely. "I'm Lord Rossley."

"Hello, lorsie," Susannah answered. "I'm Susannah and I'm three." She surveyed the newcomer with undisguised curiosity.

"Susannah." Duncan used the authoritative voice he reserved for such occasions. "You know you are supposed to do what Nurse tells you. Right?"

Slowly, his daughter turned to face him. She nodded. "But I just woke up, and I wanted to see you."

"I know, bairn, but sometimes you have to wait." He looked up at Nurse. "It is fine, Nurse. She may remain here for a few minutes."

Nurse's frown conveyed her disapproval of this plan, but she nonetheless withdrew to the corridor.

As Rossley returned to his seat, Duncan settled Susannah on his knee. Not for the first time, he wished Olivia were here to deal with situations such as this. She had been the oldest of a large and boisterous family, and she would have known every child-rearing trick there was to know.

Susannah looked up into his face. "Biscuits?" she asked.

Duncan barely restrained himself from laughing. When his daughter had a goal in mind, she pursued it with relentless zeal. She was going to be a formidable woman one day.

He looked over at his guest. "Forgive me, Lord Rossley. This will just take a minute."

"No apology necessary." Lady Tuncliffe's brother chuckled. "I am curious to see the result of this battle of wills."

Duncan returned his attention to the child. "Do you think that a little girl who runs away from her nurse deserves biscuits?"

Susannah considered this question, then nodded her head vigorously. Duncan stared back at her with what he hoped was a serious mien. She stopped nodding, gave him one last, hopeful smile, then shook her head back and forth.

"However, a good little girl who does what her nurse tells her will get a sweet at bedtime."

Susannah laughed and clapped her hands. "If I promise to be a good girl later, may I have the sweet now?"

Duncan heard a muffled snort of laughter from his guest.

"That is not the way it works, bairn."

"But what if the biscuits are all gone by bedtime?" Her brow was furrowed.

Oh, for the days when biscuits were the greatest concern in the world.

Penny piped up from across the room. "I will make sure there is a sweet left for you, lass. See, I am putting one aside for you right now." With a grand movement, she chose a toothsome-looking lemon biscuit and wrapped it in a napkin. Then she put it on the mantelpiece. Susannah's gaze followed her aunt's every move.

"So now you must do as your father

says, and go back to the nursery until later," Penny added.

Susannah glanced around the room, but no one came forward to offer another option. So she threw her arms around Duncan's neck, kissed him, and clambered down from his knee.

"Don't forget," she admonished Penny before toddling out of the room and into Nurse's waiting arms.

"Your daughter is charming," Lord Rossley said when the door had closed behind the pair.

"Thank you. She knows very well how to get her own way. Rather like your sister," he remarked. "She and I had an interesting discussion about her paintings the other day. I was trying to persuade her to hang them in her salon, but she was adamant in her refusal."

"Em's odd about her paintings," her brother observed, reaching for another biscuit. "She seems almost ashamed of them. Dashed odd. Granted, they are not in the ordinary vein — at least, not that I can tell, from the little I know of art — but they are quite striking. I have never understood why she hides them away."

"She appears to think them unseemly," Duncan said.

"That could be it. Emily is always concerned with doing the right thing," Lord Rossley said. "She even married . . ."

"She even what?" Duncan prodded. He knew it was impolite to pry, and yet he was curious.

"It is nothing." The younger man shook his head and rose. "Thank you both for your hospitality, but I should be on my way. I have several more errands to perform before I return home."

Penny and Duncan walked their guest downstairs. "Please feel free to visit any time, my lord," Penny said as he retrieved his hat from the foyer table.

"I do believe I will," he replied, and bowed politely in farewell.

"That was a pleasant break in the day," Duncan commented as they climbed the stairs back to the upper story.

"Yes, indeed." Penny's voice was far away.

Duncan smiled, but for once refrained from teasing his sister. He made a mental note, however, to inquire whether Lady Tuncliffe and her brother would consent to join them for dinner one evening. Perhaps they did not move in quite the same social circles, but Lady Tuncliffe did not seem so high in the instep that she would refuse the invitation on that basis alone.

Back at his desk, he took out the drawings for Lady Tuncliffe's kitchen. She had asked whether the proportions of the kitchen and the scullery could be rearranged. He had altered the drawings and given a copy to the workmen, but he was not certain that they would carry out his instructions properly.

"I believe I will go to Lady Tuncliffe's house later this afternoon, once I've finished this paperwork," he announced. "I want to give one of the carpenters some extra direction."

"This renovation seems to be a time-consuming project — more so than most."

"I know, but this is such an important commission for me. Everything about it must be perfect."

Why did his truthful explanation sound so hollow, even to his own ears?

Dismissing any other rationale for his frequent visits to the Tuncliffe household, he turned back to the account book on his desk. However, his mind remained fixed on the perplexing problem of Lady Tuncliffe and her artwork. What she lacked, he suspected, was confidence in her abilities. He had been the same, years ago, when he began to study architecture.

His first few commissions had cured him of his hesitancy. Perhaps a patron might bolster her self-assurance.

Mulling this over, he sharpened his pen once again and began scribbling figures.

"I have asked the workmen to move that wall slightly, which would allow more light into the scullery," Mr. McAllister said, pointing as he talked.

"Yes, I see. But would that not decrease the work space next to the hearth?" Emily tried to picture the new configuration, a task made more difficult by the fact that the kitchen was a shambles. Canvas covered a small window whose cracked glass had been removed for repairs, and a half-built shelf in one corner tilted at a drunken angle. Over everything lay a thick coating of plaster dust, which seeped down regularly from the half-finished dining room above.

"It would not reduce the work space by very much. And you could set a small table over here," the architect explained, indicating the area that would remain after the wall was moved.

"Well, the most important thing is to brighten the scullery. It is as dark as a tomb in there at present, and I feel terrible

making anyone work in such an unprom-
ising space." Emily tried to imagine the
new scullery and smiled. She had tried to
make a similar change at Tuncliffe Manor,
but Simon had scoffed at the suggestion
that they spend money to please their servants. Mr. McAllister saw nothing amiss in
the plan — or, if he did, he was too well-
bred to say so.

Well-bred he definitely was. She had
learned a little of his history during their
afternoon visits. The son of an Edinburgh
merchant, with roots in the Highlands, he
had been sent to school in England at an
early age. After attending Oxford and ap-
prenticing with an architect in Glasgow, he
had moved to London to seek grander opportunities.

She had been surprised when he had arrived at the house this afternoon, as she
had not expected him to visit for the rest of
the week. That was the reason she had
asked Alex to deliver the money to Mr.
McAllister's residence earlier in the day.

But she could not say she was sorry he
was here. As the days wore on, she was enjoying his company more and more. She
had even come to terms with her undeniable attraction to him. Since she knew she
would never marry again, she had decided

it was quite acceptable to admire him as one would admire a fine sculpture or painting. As long as no one knew, no one would be harmed.

Freed of the need to hunt or be hunted that had made her season such a misery, she could simply appreciate him.

It was delightful.

As she watched him move about the large room, raking his hand through his ginger hair as he looked up at the tops of the windows, she found herself longing for a sketch pad. Something about the arch of his arm cried out to be captured on paper.

"I have been thinking some more about your paintings," Mr. McAllister remarked, taking a measuring tape from the pocket of his coat.

Emily's heart sank. She hoped he was not about to argue with her again about her decision to hang them in her bedroom. It was the one serious point of contention that had arisen between them.

"Yes?" She tried to keep her voice light.

"You mentioned that you have dozens in storage at Stonecourt. It is unlikely you will have the space to hang so many artworks in the private rooms of this home. Have you ever considered offering any of them for sale?"

"Selling them?" Despite her resolve to be calm, Emily heard a note of panic creep into her voice.

"I know — you fear those rioters we spoke of the other day would spread their unrest through the whole of London." He shook his head in mock surprise. "You are most civic-minded to consider the public welfare above your personal gain!"

Despite her discomfort, Emily laughed. Never had she met a man with such an engaging sense of the ridiculous. "I do what I can."

Mr. McAllister's smile turned sympathetic. "Seriously, I can understand how difficult it would be to part with your paintings."

"Yes, it would be hard, but that is not the reason I resist the idea. It is just that, to sell them, I would need to reveal the fact that I had painted them. I know your feelings on that subject," she added in a rush, anxious to forestall the objection she sensed was rising to his lips. "However, I must assure you that an artist's life is the last thing I desire. I was not raised to be comfortable in such a position."

Mr. McAllister was silent for a moment. Then he asked, in a gentle voice, "What did Lord Tuncliffe think of your paintings?"

Whatever she had expected as a reaction to her outburst, such a question was not it. What on earth was she to say that would not be disloyal?

"Remember, I knew your husband years ago. He did not, if you will forgive me, seem to be much inclined toward artistic pursuits."

That was understating the facts to a great degree.

"He was not interested in the arts, true. But he was not much given to commenting on my paintings," she said, neglecting to add that she had been careful to keep them out of his sight.

Suddenly, and with a ferocity that astonished her, she longed to pour out the story of her years with Simon to this kind man. Perhaps because he had mentioned that he had known Simon, she felt that, somehow, she would not be betraying Simon by being honest.

But a betrayal it would be. She had married Simon — had promised to love him for better or for worse — and part of that promise included honoring his memory.

"I have a proposition to make to you," Mr. McAllister said, startling her out of her musings.

"Yes?"

"Are you still interested in altering the study for use as a studio?"

Her heart quickened at the very idea. "But I thought you said it would not be possible."

"It will require a number of hours of extra work on my part to draw up the plans. But I would be willing to absorb that cost, and to split the cost of the materials and the workers' time, in exchange for a favor."

She had enough money left over in her small budget to cover those costs. But what on earth could Emily do for Mr. McAllister in exchange for so generous an offer? "A favor?" she echoed.

"I would very much like you to paint a portrait of my daughter, Susannah."

Emily sat down heavily on a small stool by the hearth, so thunderstruck was she by this request. She had never painted a posed portrait before, nor had she ever taken a child as her subject.

She had also had no idea that Mr. McAllister had a child. Why had he never mentioned her — or his wife?

"Your daughter?" she heard herself say in a faint voice.

"Yes. I would very much like to have a true likeness of her. She is the image of her

73

mother — except, of course, that Susannah has the misfortune to have inherited my red hair."

"I did not know you were married, Mr. McAllister."

"I am not any longer." He sat down on a stool on the opposite side of the hearth, and stared out the small window above the sink before continuing. "My wife Olivia died suddenly a few months after Susannah was born." His voice was muted, as though he had swallowed a mouthful of cotton.

Sympathy pierced Emily. She knew instantly that Mr. McAllister's relationship with his late wife had been nothing like her fraught marriage to Simon.

"I am so sorry, Mr. McAllister. Had she been ill for a long time?"

"No, that is the dreadful thing about it. She was always the picture of health, and she loved to walk." He paused, as if gathering his thoughts. "I was working on a project in Shropshire, designing a new wing for a small country estate. We had spent a great deal of time apart, so she decided to accompany me. Susannah was only an infant, so we left her in London, in the care of her nurse."

He stared at the wall, as though he were

watching a play that only he could see. "While I was meeting with the client, Olivia stayed in the village where we had taken rooms. One afternoon, she went out for a walk and became lost. The weather changed, and she was caught in a violent rainstorm."

His voice grew softer, until Emily could barely hear it. "When I returned to the inn, the innkeeper said she had been gone for several hours. When I finally found her, she was drenched to the skin and shivering. I brought her back, but she developed a wracking cough and a high fever."

He looked down at his hands, folded together in his lap. "Two weeks later, she was dead."

Emily did not know what to say. "Were you married long?"

"Two years, but we had known each other from childhood. She lived near my family in Edinburgh." He raised his head. "She was the only young lady I knew who could put up with my antics. If I had not married her, I would have remained a bachelor."

"I am certain that is not true," Emily said, meaning it. "And I am sorry that I have provoked such unpleasant memories."

"No, I am the one who should apologize," Mr. McAllister said, rubbing his hands together and rising from his stool. "You asked me a straightforward question, and did not ask to hear the entire tale of my life."

"Is that why you have never mentioned your daughter before — because you did not wish to discuss your wife?"

"Yes. It is not that I am wracked with grief — my long tale to the contrary. I simply find it easier not to speak of personal matters with my clients. Most clients."

"I understand." Emily refused to ponder the meaning of his last comment.

Mr. McAllister shook a finger at her in mock reproach. "You have not answered my question. Would you be willing to paint Susannah?"

"How old is your daughter?"

"She is three, and that could be a problem — I am not certain that she could sit still long enough for you to capture her. She does, however, respond well to bribery." A brief smile flitted across his face. "I think you would like her. She certainly enjoyed meeting your brother this afternoon."

"I love children, Mr. McAllister, and I would like to meet your daughter. But I am not certain I am the best choice to paint her. Would you not prefer to engage an artist with more experience in portraiture?"

Mr. McAllister chuckled. "The budgets of young architects, Lady Tuncliffe, are as constrained as those of young widows. My funds, at the moment, would not allow me to commission a portrait from someone such as John Constable or Charles Walsh. You would be doing me a favor by taking this on. This barter would allow us each to attain something we strongly desire but can ill afford."

It was so tempting. "But my style is nothing like that of the artists you mentioned," she said. "I have had no formal training, aside from some desultory lessons at the school for young ladies I once attended. I am not sure —"

"Your style is perfect for Susannah — lighthearted and joyful," Mr. McAllister cut in. "You will understand when you meet her — she has the energy of ten grown men."

Emily hesitated. Could she paint a posed portrait?

Could she keep a lively child amused enough to sit still?

Could she get over her fear of working in view of others? Most of her other paintings had been created stealthily, without their subjects' knowledge.

A vision of the renovated study, flooded with light, appeared in her mind's eye. A place where she could keep her brushes, canvases, and palettes safe from others' notice.

A place where she could be as independent as ever she had dreamed.

To get that, she could do this.

"Yes, Mr. McAllister," she said. "Yes, I would be honored to paint a portrait of your daughter."

As they left the kitchen, Emily reflected once again that Mr. McAllister was skilled in bending others to his will. Despite her vocal protests, he had convinced her to do the one thing she had told him she would never do — paint for profit.

Would she spend her life doing as others wished?

As she began to despair at the thought, she brought herself up short. She was not doing as he wanted simply because he had asked her to. She was getting something she desired in return — her studio.

Independence would not come all at once, she told herself as she climbed the dusty stairs toward the ground floor. Sometimes, one must compromise.

Five

Emily squinted at the canvas and tilted her head to get a better look. No, something was still not quite right about the eyes.

She glanced next at Susannah. The little girl was being remarkably good, given that stillness was not her strong suit. But she had the restless look that Emily had come to realize presaged an imminent bolt for freedom.

Miss McAllister crossed the room and peered over her shoulder. "My, the painting is coming along marvelously, Lady Tuncliffe! It is very like her."

"Thank you." Emily still felt awkward about working in the open, but if she had to have an audience, she could not have chosen a better one than Miss McAllister. The architect's sister was pleasant, funny, and eminently good company — very like her brother, in fact. Emily and she often spent companionable afternoons together in the McAllister sitting room, with Emily painting as Miss McAllister wrote letters or did needlework.

"I am still frustrated in capturing her

eyes, however," Emily added. "She has this pretty look when she laughs that I so want to reproduce, and yet it is so fleeting."

"I can make her laugh," Miss McAllister whispered.

"Susannah?" she called to her niece. The child perked up. "Remember the bunny we saw in the park?"

Immediately, the little girl chortled, her whole face alight. "With the flop-ears?"

Penny nodded, as Emily seized a pad and pencil and began to sketch the lines of Susannah's face.

"Remember how we followed him down to the pond?" Penny asked.

"And there was another bunny there. Two bunnies!"

As she sketched, Emily marveled at the simplicity of the child's reactions. With children, life was so uncomplicated: night and day, black and white, good and bad. It was one of the many reasons she loved being around them. One of the many reasons she had so wanted children of her own.

She shut the door on that line of thought, and returned her attention to her young subject.

"And what did he do when he saw the other bunny?"

Susannah wrinkled her forehead. Then she grinned, and Emily's pencil flew once more. "They rubbed noses!" she crowed, clapping her hands.

Miss McAllister kept the child reminiscing for a few more minutes, until Emily put down the pad. "I think that has done the trick. I should be able to fix that aspect of the painting quite nicely now. Thank you, Miss McAllister."

"Please, Lady Tuncliffe, do call me Penny. I feel I have known you for years, and all my friends call me Penny."

"You must call me Emily, then!" Emily exclaimed, pleased and touched that the younger woman considered her a friend. She had had so few intimates since her marriage to Simon. "Are you certain you would not prefer me to call you Penelope?"

Her companion's mouth drew down in a moue of distaste. "I have no idea why my parents settled on so grandiose a name for me. They chose perfectly sensible names for the boys — one cannot complain that either 'Neil' or 'Duncan' is too high-flown. I have never liked my full name — sometimes, I even forget to respond to it!"

"We are alike in that respect," Emily replied. "I have never fully adapted to being called Lady Tuncliffe. It sounds like the

81

name of a much older, more serious person than I."

Penny circled behind Emily's chair once more and glanced at her sketch of Susannah. "You have a remarkable talent. I cannot believe you produced such a detailed drawing in just a few minutes."

Emily could feel a warm blush rising up her neck. "Thank you," she murmured, averting her eyes.

"You should not be embarrassed by the truth!"

"It is just that I am unused to people observing me at work. Despite your brother's reassurances, I cannot help but think that painting portraits in public is not exactly ladylike."

"Don't be silly! It is perfectly respectable." Penny moved back to her seat on the sofa. "There were female painters centuries ago. An Italian lady named Lavinia Fontana was awarded public commissions during the Renaissance. And her countrywoman, Sofonisba Anguissola, became a court painter to one of the Spanish monarchs — Queen Isabella of Valois, I believe it was. She even attracted the praise of Michelangelo!"

"Where did you learn all this? I have never heard tell of it." Emily was fascinated, but she kept her eyes on her easel. Susannah would beg to escape any minute, and Emily wanted to execute a few last brushstrokes first.

"I was very fortunate. My father put great store by education. I received instruction in Latin, Greek, art, and mathematics from my brothers' tutors, one of whom was mad about Italian painting. Neil was not much interested — to this day, he would scarcely know a painting from a pony — but Duncan and I used to borrow the tutor's books."

"How wonderful!"

"Did you not have tutors?"

"No. I had several governesses, who were very kind but who believed that sewing and household management were really all a female needed to know. I did attend a school for young ladies when I was older, but we learned little of ancient languages and nothing of mathematics. One of the teachers instructed us in watercolors for several years. Fortunately, her brother was an artist, so she was able to teach me the basics of mixing paint. The rest I determined through trial and error."

"So you have largely taught yourself?" Penny's voice was admiring.

Emily nodded. "I spent much time alone

when I lived in Hampshire, and I found the work relaxing."

Below, she heard the front door open and close. "How is the masterpiece progressing?" Mr. McAllister's voice boomed up the stairway.

Emily's heart skipped a beat. Penny had said her brother was meeting a new client this afternoon and might not be home until the early evening. It was an unexpected treat to have his company.

She was amazed at her growing fascination with the lanky architect. In her six and twenty years, she had never been so intrigued by a man — certainly not by her late husband. She found herself endlessly curious to know everything about him: what books he read, what foods he enjoyed, what he thought about the issues of the day.

But more than that, she found that she responded to him as she had never responded to another human being, her every sense heightened whenever he was near. It was rather the way she felt when she was painting, she realized.

And yet, not quite.

Emily was wise enough to realize that she could quite easily fall in love with Mr. McAllister. But that, she knew, would be the height of folly. It would be improper to become involved with a man so soon after leaving off mourning clothes. In any case, she had no right to any man's affection.

"I have had better success today, with your sister's help," she replied as she heard him enter the room.

Further conversation was precluded for the moment, however, as Susannah scrambled down from her perch on a high dining room chair and launched herself across the floor.

"Father!" she cried, hugging his leg.

"Good afternoon, bairn," he said, picking her up and swinging her in his arms until she shrieked in delight.

"What does that mean — 'bairn'?" Emily asked.

He stopped spinning for a minute, drawing a squeal of protest from his daughter. "It means 'child.' Just an endearment."

"It is a shame you seldom use Scottish words. I enjoy learning them."

"Someday I will read you some Robert Burns poetry, but only if I can locate a Scots dictionary first. My ken is rusty."

"Ken?"

"Knowledge. It is also a verb, 'to know' or 'to understand.' "

He lifted the little girl high above his head, prompting an even higher-pitched squeal. "Have you been behaving yourself for Lady Tuncliffe?"

"She has been very good and very patient," Emily said, smiling. Mr. McAllister and Susannah were such easy companions. She could not have imagined Simon being so natural with a child, even had they been able to have one. The few times they had been around other people's children, he had dismissed them as smelly, noisy creatures.

" 'Good' sounds like my Susannah, but 'patient' is not normally a word I associate with her," Mr. McAllister replied, tickling his daughter under the chin before setting her down. "Should you be getting back in your chair?" he asked the child.

Susannah frowned. "I sat in the chair a lot today." She looked up at Emily, a mute plea in her eyes.

"So you did, and I think we have finished for now," Emily said. "Perhaps Cook might be persuaded to give you a biscuit if you —"

Before she could finish the sentence, Susannah had scampered off in the direction of the kitchen.

"And you say that I spoil her!" Penny exclaimed, looking at Mr. McAllister.

"She is very like my brother was at that age," Emily said. "Extremely fond of her sweets."

"At that age?" Penny asked, laughing. "I would say he is still fond of biscuits and puddings."

Emily and Alex had taken up the habit of dining with the McAllisters once or twice a week, and Alex also occasionally accompanied his sister when she worked on the portrait. Emily suspected, however, that his interest in Miss McAllister was much deeper than his interest in the painting.

"Well, I suppose my work is finished for this afternoon," Emily said, leaning down to pick up a brush that had fallen on the cloth covering the floor.

As she straightened up, she almost bumped the top of her head on Mr. McAllister's chin. He had moved behind her to look at something on the easel. Hastily, she sat down on a small chair.

"My apologies, Lady Tuncliffe," he said, backing away slightly.

She almost asked him to call her Emily, as she had invited his sister to do, but the words died on her tongue. It was one thing for ladies to address each other by their

Christian names, but another thing altogether to invite a gentleman to take such a liberty. Besides, it would be unwise to create any greater intimacy than they already shared. Friends could be friends and still be formal.

"I was just examining these sketches of Susannah," he murmured. "You have captured her very well."

Emily remained very still, sensing how near Mr. McAllister was. His breath was warm on her hair, and the air was scented with the faint aroma of sandalwood soap that always surrounded him.

When she became aware of the ticking of the small carriage clock on the mantelpiece, she realized that she had not responded to his compliment about the sketches.

"You may have them when I am done, if you like," she said in a rush.

"I just may take you up on that offer, Lady Tuncliffe. They might make admirable advertisements for your work, should you ever decide to take my advice and solicit other commissions."

Her pleasure in his regard ebbed away. Why would he not stop pressing her to become a professional artist? It was ironic, really. She had been distraught when

Simon had derided her efforts as unworthy of public display, and now she was annoyed because Mr. McAllister would not stop urging her to share them.

Why did men always want to run one's life?

"I thank you for your advice, Mr. McAllister, but I believe you already know my opinions on this subject." She hoped her voice was suitably cool.

"I have remarkable powers of persuasion. Failing that, there are always the leg irons in the scullery. I believe we have a rack in the attic, as well. Came with the house."

She twisted around in her chair to look at him, and immediately regretted her action. She was close enough to touch his face, which was disconcerting. "I have made up my mind."

"Minds can be changed."

"Not mine. Not on this issue." *Let me be,* she prayed silently.

He gave her one of those intent looks that seemed to turn her entire being inside out for his inspection. "We will see," he said, moving away from her chair at last.

She breathed a quiet sigh of relief and collected the last of her supplies. Suddenly, she was eager to be on her way and to avoid another debate with Mr. McAllister.

Why would he not simply accept her views? Obviously, she still had much to learn about asserting her wishes.

Duncan peered into the window of a Bond Street shop, admiring a blue hat. It would look well on Lady Tuncliffe, he thought — it was just the shade to match her eyes.

This new interest in millinery was odd, and he could not seem to stop thinking about the shy viscountess. He had given no other woman more than a passing glance since the day he had met Olivia, almost two decades ago.

And the strange thing was, he reflected as he moved away from the shop, that Lady Tuncliffe was nothing like his late wife. Olivia had been bubbly, confident, and witty — always the bright and charming star around which any party had revolved.

As time passed, he found that he could usually think of Olivia with gratitude and love, rather than grief. That moment in Lady Tuncliffe's kitchen had been a rarity — he had not shown his feelings so brazenly since the day Olivia was buried. But there was something about Lady Tuncliffe that encouraged one to talk. She was so still. Like a calm pond, he thought.

At the thought, he chuckled. He was not a man generally given to such flights of fancy as comparing women to bodies of water.

As he strolled up the street, he continued to ponder the question of why he found Lady Tuncliffe so appealing when she differed so from his headstrong, passionate wife.

Or perhaps she was not so different. Lady Tuncliffe's refusal to hang her artworks in her salon showed that she could be headstrong. And the paintings revealed a depth of emotion that she was otherwise careful to conceal. In her pictures, even the humblest subjects were imbued with life and light. He thought of the painting of the washerwoman pegging out her laundry, her shoulders strong and her hair whipped by the breeze. He recalled the bold colors of the painting: the woman's crimson apron and an apple-green tablecloth on the line.

But if Lady Tuncliffe had such depths of feeling, how could she have borne a marriage to one such as Simon Wallace? Over tea one afternoon in Berkeley Square, she had told him that the marriage had been an arranged one. But when he had asked whether she had been happy in the union, she had merely said, "As happy as most wives are — or husbands, for that matter," and changed the subject.

As they had become better friends, he had given her openings to vent any frustrations she might have had about her marriage. But not once did she indicate that she had been anything but content.

Unless Simon Wallace had become a different man since their days at school, Duncan could not believe this to be the case. But why would she conceal the truth?

So intent was he on these musings that he almost did not hear someone calling his name until he practically tripped over the gentleman in question.

"Duncan McAllister, have you gone quite deaf?"

On the pavement before him stood the most elegant — and ridiculous — fop. His shirt points were sharp and high enough to be considered lethal weapons, while the fabric of his scarlet and gold waistcoat would not have looked out of place as a wall covering in a Covent Garden house of ill repute. Atop it he wore a dark blue velvet coat with elaborate frogs. His skintight yellow pantaloons made one wonder whether he could breathe in comfort.

Although Duncan had not seen him in more than a decade, since they had been schoolboys at Harrow, he would have known Piers Sherrington anywhere. Not only did he retain his boyish looks, but he was also the subject of frequent illustrations in the London newspapers. Even Duncan, whose tastes in books rarely moved beyond political biographies and architectural treatises, recognized one of England's most famous poets.

"Sherrington!" he cried, clapping the other man on the back. "What a pleasure to see you!"

He meant the words. The two schoolboys had had little in common, Piers being relentlessly literary while Duncan had preferred the sports field. And yet, they had struck up an odd fellowship of outcasts, teased as both had been by bullies such as Simon Wallace.

"It is indeed wonderful to see you, too, my old confrere," Piers replied. "It is the friends we make in our youth who sustain us throughout life's travails."

Piers's manner of speech had always been flowery. Duncan had learned years ago not to pay it much heed.

"You have certainly succeeded in your field," Duncan said. "My congratulations."

"Thank you. It is a joy indeed to make one's living from one's most cherished pursuit. And what of you? Did I hear correctly that you are an architect?"

"You did. Like you, I am blessed to have great satisfaction in my work."

"My wife and I have been thinking of adding a portico to our country house," Piers remarked. "This meeting is quite serendipitous! Could I entice you to share a glass or two of port with me at Brooks's, where we could discuss the matter?"

"By all means." Silently, Duncan rejoiced. The client he had met with earlier in the week, while initially enthusiastic about working with him, had later informed him that he had accepted another architect's bid instead. It was not the first time such a thing had happened, and Duncan had tried everything — different styles, lower fees — to counteract the trend. So far, nothing had worked. Piers's offer of work was more enticing than his old acquaintance could possibly know.

It was a short walk from Bond Street to Brooks's in St. James's. Looking around the premises, Duncan realized he should probably be spending more time at the club, to which he nominally belonged. Even at this early hour, it was full of the cream of the *ton,* many bent on emptying their pockets in the most spectacular way possible. Several, including two members of Parliament and a florid earl, were engaged in obviously deep play around a faro table.

He and Sherrington settled into butter-soft leather chairs in a quiet corner. After an hour of discussing the relative virtues of Doric and Corinthian columns, sketching ideas on a sheaf of foolscap, and downing rather more wine than Duncan was used to consuming in the middle of the afternoon, the two began to reminisce about their school days.

"A dreadful place, Harrow," Piers said, signaling the waiter for another bottle of port. "Truly, I have never been so happy to shake the dust of an establishment off my boots. If it had not been for you and a few others, I would have gone mad. Speaking of fellow students, had you heard that Willoughby married an heiress last year?"

Spencer Willoughby had been another of their informal clan of outsiders. His sins had consisted of a marked disinterest in cricket and a fascination with science — neither inclination widely understood at Harrow.

"Yes, I run into him occasionally in Gentleman Jackson's rooms. Say, you should join me there some afternoon — we could do a little sparring."

Piers recoiled in horror. "Pugilism? I should say not, my friend. I cannot risk injuring my hands, for then my livelihood would be gone. I am surprised you engage in such sport, seeing as you need manual dexterity in your profession, as well."

"It is a very handy diversion when one needs to release one's frustrations," Duncan remarked, recalling with sudden vividness the long nights he had spent at Jackson's academy just after Olivia died, taking out his anger on a defenseless punching bag or on unwary sparring partners. He was glad those days were long behind him.

"I will take your word for it and decline with thanks," said Piers, accepting the new bottle of wine from the waiter. He poured himself a glass and then waggled the bottle at Duncan, who shook his head. "However, I would like to maintain our acquaintance, now that we have renewed it. My wife and I are hosting a small soirée tomorrow, and we would be delighted if you would attend. I have not even asked — are you married?"

"I was," Duncan answered. "My wife

passed away three years ago, and my sister now keeps house for me."

"I am very sorry to hear about your wife's death," said Piers with a sympathetic shake of his head. "Please feel free to bring your sister to the party as well. It will be an intimate gathering of some forty or so people."

Duncan thought wryly that his and Piers's definitions of "intimate" varied somewhat. But then, Sherrington had married a famously rich woman. And from the discussion of the proposed portico, their home sounded enormous.

"Most of the guests will be artistic sorts — painters, writers, composers, and such. The artist Charles Walsh will be there, and I hear that he is thinking of adding a wing to Walsh House. Perhaps you may secure some new commissions!"

"I would be pleased to attend," said Duncan, who would have accepted his friend's offer even without the enticement of work. But that possibility made the invitation doubly difficult to refuse.

And then there was the fact that Charles Walsh would be at the party. Perhaps Duncan could learn more about the market for unusual artworks — something he could use to encourage Lady Tuncliffe in her work.

She had not responded well to his encouragement so far. But the more ammunition he had, the more likely he would be to win the battle. It frustrated him that she could not recognize her talent as the means to a more secure income. He had also deplored the waste of any talent ever since his brother Neil had forsaken his true avocation, the clergy, for life behind the counter of their father's store.

He felt strongly about Lady Tuncliffe's artistic potential. But did he really want to fight with her again?

Well, it would do no harm to meet Walsh and these other artists. He could decide later what to do with the information.

"Bring along a contract for the work we have discussed — I would like to proceed as soon as possible," Sherrington was saying.

"Are you certain you wish to move so fast? Do you not wish to get other estimates?"

"Your ideas seem sound, and I much prefer working with friends to dealing with strangers."

Duncan barely dared to hope that this commission would materialize, but it seemed promising. "I will have the paperwork with me tomorrow. Here is to renewed friendships," he said, raising his near empty glass and touching it to Piers's full one.

"An admirable toast. To renewed friendships, indeed."

Six

"The background is coming along nicely," Mr. McAllister observed as he looked at the portrait. He was standing in the middle of the room as Emily worked on the painting. A safe distance away.

Thank goodness.

She was pleased with her progress, since she had been working steadily for several weeks. Her afternoons at the McAllister house in Chelsea gave her a welcome respite from the dust and chaos in Berkeley Square. She was still glad she had moved into her residence right away, but she had to concede that the house was not restful.

"The background is the simple part," she replied, not turning from her work. "It is likely that I will need her to sit for me only once or twice more before the portrait is done. I suspect she is glad that I did not need her services today."

"Oh, I would not be so sure. As much as she complains, she adores being the center of attention, the wee imp."

Emily smiled. It always charmed her when proof of Mr. McAllister's Scottish origins crept into his speech.

Behind her, she heard him move to the sofa and open the newspaper. She wondered why he was home so often during the day. He had seemed to spend a lot of time at her home during the early stages of the renovations. Surely he had similar responsibilities with other clients?

In all likelihood, he was just in a lull between commissions. She had heard him mention that a few projects had fallen through. It was pleasant to have his company while she painted, especially since he had stopped badgering her on the issue of accepting commissions of her own.

The only drawback to his presence was the fact that he sometimes distracted her from her work.

Today, however, she was absorbed in the painting. There was a troublesome curtain behind Susannah's chair that Emily was having trouble rendering realistically. As she was shading one of the folds, she heard a knock at the front door.

"That could be Charles Walsh," Mr. McAllister said in a casual voice.

"Charles *Walsh?*" In her shock, Emily dropped her brush to the floor cloth, the drapery forgotten. She turned to stare at Mr. McAllister. "Charles Walsh of the Royal Academy?"

"Yes, that is right. He is an acquaintance of an old school chum of mine, Piers Sherrington, who may accompany him today."

The significance of the second name penetrated Emily's suddenly agitated mind. "The *poet?*"

"Yes." Mr. McAllister gave her an infuriating smile. "Piers and I encountered each other on Bond Street last week, and he has commissioned me to design a portico."

"Congratulations."

The architect took a deep breath. "Walsh, whom I met at a soirée of Sherrington's, is interested in adding a wing to his house. He mentioned he might come around this afternoon to discuss it, but we did not make a definite appointment."

One look into Mr. McAllister's wide, hazel eyes told Emily all she needed to know. Like her, he was a poor liar. He averted his gaze.

"And you felt no need to tell me that one of England's leading painters might happen to visit this afternoon while I was at work?"

"You were busy — I saw no need to interrupt you."

Emily's mind was a whirlwind of emotions as she heard Libby answer the door. Two male voices echoed in the foyer.

"It was unkind of you to set me up this way, Mr. McAllister, when you know how much I abhor an audience," Emily spat. The riot of emotions had settled until only one remained: blind anger.

"I know you would never accept an introduction to Walsh directly. So I thought —"

"I know what you thought!" She kept her voice low with the greatest difficulty. "You thought you could get me to do what you think best by tricking me into it. Just like a man!"

Before Emily could continue however, Libby stepped through the doorway. "Mr. McAllister, sir? Mr. Sherrington and Mr. Walsh are here to see you."

"Show them in, Libby."

"You cannot . . . I cannot . . . oh my heavens!" Emily exclaimed, feeling ill. She had time to say nothing else, however, before the two celebrated gentlemen walked through the door of Mr. McAllister's modest sitting room.

"McAllister, good to see you again," boomed the bluff older man, extending his hand. "I am looking forward to hearing more about your plans for the new wing."

"What a charming abode you have fashioned for yourself," the man she recognized as Piers Sherrington exclaimed. "It is a veritable bijou!"

"Well, it is hardly a palace, but I could not afford the household help it requires to run Carlton House." Mr. McAllister laughed. "It has an unappealing façade and some strange crannies, but the price was within my budget. One day, I would like to design my own home."

"And so you will," Mr. Sherrington said. "But here we stand talking, and you have not introduced me to this lovely lady. Is she another of your sisters?"

If only, Emily thought. Then she would be well within her rights to box the architect's ears.

"No, this is Lady Tuncliffe," Mr. McAllister said.

Emily gave thanks for the governesses who had trained her to remain calm in any social situation. As if animated by clockwork, she rose from her chair and smiled at the two gentlemen.

"Lady Tuncliffe?" Mr. Sherrington mused. "Are you not the sister of Lady Langdon?"

Emily assented that she was.

"I once thought I might have a chance of

marrying your sister, back in the summer before she accepted Langdon's suit," the poet said with a theatrical sigh.

Emily suppressed a smile. Although she and Mr. Sherrington had never met, she had heard most of the details of his suit from Clarissa — and the rest from their sister Lucy. Mr. Sherrington, it appeared, had lost interest in Clarissa's hand at almost the exact moment he had learned that her dowry was not as large as he had believed.

Emily let Mr. Sherrington keep to his version of the story, however, as she had more important concerns. The way Mr. Walsh was looking at her painting, for one.

"That is an intriguing portrait, Lady Tuncliffe," the great artist said, cocking his gray head to one side as he examined it. "You have a deft and unique style."

Mr. Sherrington moved away to converse with Mr. McAllister.

Emily pondered Mr. Walsh's comment. Was it a gentle way of saying that she was an untalented dilettante? Or did he really think her work remarkable? She could not decide.

"The energy that emanates from the child's face is extraordinary," he said. "With whom did you study?"

"I have had little formal training, sir. My instruction has been limited to a few lessons in watercolors with governesses and the teachers at my small school."

"A few lessons, and you have achieved this level? My dear, you have a natural talent! It is unfortunate that you did not have the opportunity to study further, and that you cannot join the Royal Academy."

"Unfortunate, perhaps, but not surprising. Such opportunities are rarely open to women, which is eminently sensible. Few women have professions and even fewer would consider painting a respectable one — for themselves, that is," she added hastily, lest Mr. Walsh think that she found all painters disreputable.

"True enough," he said, still eyeing the painting. "Do you mix your own paints?"

She nodded. "I am not certain I am doing so in the correct fashion, but the results please me."

"It is a difficult process, and you have done well. Have you painted many other works?"

Emily paused. Mr. McAllister knew about the paintings stored at Stonecourt, so she could hardly deny their existence. "A few, yes. Nothing of great import."

"I have seen several of them," Mr.

McAllister piped up from the other side of the room, where he had appeared to be deep in discussion with Mr. Sherrington. "They are beautiful, and quite unlike anything I have encountered in a Royal Academy exhibition."

"Is that so?" Mr. Walsh stroked his beard.

Emily noted, irrelevantly, that he looked neither disreputable nor bohemian — although his friend Mr. Sherrington appeared rather dissolute.

Mr. Walsh reached into his pocket and withdrew a brushed silver case. Opening it, he took out a card and gave it to her.

"My dear, if you wish an opinion on your other works, please do not hesitate to call on me. I would be interested to see them."

As she took the card, Emily struggled to remain upright without gripping the frame of the easel for support. Charles Walsh wanted to see her paintings!

Just as quickly as the euphoria had flooded her veins, however, it receded. Attention would bring her hobby into public view. She would be ridiculed among the *ton,* where painting was viewed on a par with acting or operatic singing — something to enjoy but not something to do, es-

107

pecially for money.

People would think she had to work, that Simon had left her nothing.

Emily said nothing of all this, however, merely accepted Mr. Walsh's card with thanks. After he had excused himself to discuss plans for his renovation with Mr. McAllister, Mr. Sherrington joined her once more.

"Do you have any influence with your obstinate friend?" the poet asked, nodding toward Mr. McAllister.

"None that anyone would notice," she muttered. Obstinate was an excellent word. Trust a poet to have well-honed diction.

Mr. Sherrington sighed. "That is a pity, because I have just spent the better part of ten minutes trying to convince him to part with that exquisite vase on the shelf above his desk. But he will not hear of it!"

Emily glanced at the item in question. "Why, I have been to this house a dozen times, and I have never paid much heed to the piece. What is it that intrigues you?"

"It is a quite unusual item from Delft, but its rarity is not its attraction. Rather, I believe it is an exact match for a vase my wife has in her sitting room. She is very fond of it, and I would like to give her another so that she could place one at each end of her mantelpiece."

"That is a kind thought, sir. However, if Mr. McAllister is reluctant to sell, I doubt you will be able to change his mind. He can be stubborn."

"Yes, but every man has his price. I will see whether I can discern his."

The talk moved from pottery to literature and mutual acquaintances. Emily supposed she should excuse herself and return home, but she had no intention of doing so. She had a few things she wanted to discuss with Mr. McAllister after his guests departed.

When Sherrington and Walsh had left, Duncan turned to Lady Tuncliffe. At the minute, she reminded him not at all of a calm pond. A seacoast roiling in a thunderstorm came closer to the mark.

Perhaps some gentle encouragement was in order.

"Mr. Walsh was interested in your work, Lady Tuncliffe!" he said, with a heartiness he did not feel. "You must be pleased."

"I am most displeased," she said, as she put her brushes into a paint-stained canvas bag and yanked the drawstrings closed. "How could you put me in such an intolerable position?"

"It was for your own good," he replied, piqued at her lack of gratitude.

"How can becoming a public laughingstock possibly be good for me?" she asked, her voice like a knife.

"You need not be a laughingstock! There are many women who pursue artistic careers, under their own names or anonymously. Look at Miss Austen. She kept her identity secret for years! And Mrs. Edgeworth is well regarded."

"Writing is at least a moderately respectable profession. But even men find it hard to be painters. Why, I once heard that Mr. Constable's own father discouraged him from pursuing a painting career."

"If every man in Britain listened to his father when choosing a career, we would be a nation of desperate wretches!" Duncan shot back.

"It is different for a man! I am a woman, without the protection of a husband or a fortune. I cannot afford to be unusual."

"You cannot afford to waste your talents, either. There are probably hundreds of struggling painters who would sell their souls to have a tenth of the talent you possess. And you are keeping it selfishly to yourself."

"That is my choice!" Lady Tuncliffe shouted. Duncan was so startled to hear her raise her voice that he almost forgot to pay attention to what she was saying.

"I have spent enough of my life listening to men tell me what to do. For once, I will do what I choose to do." Picking up her bag and sketchpad, she strode from the room.

"What men? Simon?" He followed her downstairs and into the foyer. "Simon Wallace was an ass!"

"Simon Wallace was my husband." Her voice was low and fierce. "And I will thank you not to speak ill of the dead."

"You cannot stand there and tell me that you truly loved one such as he." Duncan was surprised to realize that he was holding his breath as he waited for her reply. Surely she would say that he was right?

"I will tell you nothing. You do not deserve an answer, as that would imply respect. And you have shown this afternoon that you have no respect for me." Libby had hurried into the foyer, a questioning look in her eyes. "If you would be so good as to bring me my mantle and gloves, Libby, I will be leaving."

She returned her gaze to Duncan. "If

that suits you, Mr. McAllister."

This was a new and unpleasant side of Lady Tuncliffe. "It is of no matter to me. You seem eager to do as you like, and I have no interest in standing in your way."

He turned and stalked back up the stairs to the sitting room. That would be the last time he would try to encourage the stubborn Lady Tuncliffe to do anything. She could spend her life painting door frames for all that it mattered to him.

As he strode back into the sitting room and sank into the chair by his desk, he sighed. Despite his bluster, Lady Tuncliffe's choices did matter to him, much to his annoyance.

Dismissing all thoughts of the viscountess, he picked up the notes he had made regarding Mr. Walsh's renovation. He had to start concentrating on his work and stop wasting his energies on other matters. Perhaps Walsh's commission would not disintegrate to ashes before the contract was signed.

Unfortunately, no amount of calculating and sketching seemed to erase the image of Lady Tuncliffe's furious, heart-shaped face from his mind. Finally, in frustration, Duncan abandoned his desk and went out for a vigorous walk along the Chelsea Embankment. There was nothing like physical exercise to clear the brain.

A few days later, Emily was back in the McAllisters' sitting room. She had let Susannah run off, deciding that the main portion of the portrait was as finished as she was capable of making it. In the end, she was satisfied with the way she had captured the child's sparkling personality. In the picture, Susannah sat on the edge of her chair, a gleam in her eye. She looked ready to bound off the furniture and out of the frame, like one of the rabbits she adored.

Now, Emily was putting the finishing touches on the background. After a number of false starts, she had fixed the problem with the troublesome drape. All that remained was to shade a patch of sunlight falling from a nearby window, so that it provided the proper counterpoint to a darker corner of the room.

On the sofa behind her, Alex and Penny were chatting. Out of the corner of her eye, she thought she saw Alex holding Miss McAllister's hand, but when she swiveled her gaze in their direction, they were sitting as decorously as possible, with at least several inches of space between them.

Emily smiled. The last thing she wanted to do was to interfere with their happiness. Alex almost always accompanied her now to her painting sessions, as the afternoons gave him the opportunity to court Miss McAllister in perfectly respectable surroundings. Who better to serve as chaperone than his widowed sister?

Miss McAllister's widowed brother might make an equally good chaperone, Emily reflected, but he was rarely about the house of late. Since their argument the previous week, she had scarcely seen him. Once, he had been leaving the house just as she had arrived. They had wished each other a good afternoon but said nothing more.

Emily was still angry with him for his high-handed attempt to change her mind about becoming a professional artist. And yet, she very much missed his company in the afternoons. He had been a constructive critic of her work on the portrait. More than that, he had been uniquely cheering. The rooms felt empty without him.

She laid down her brush with a sigh.

"Frustrated, Em?" Alex asked.

"A little. I have stayed longer than usual, and I do not think I will be able to get this last detail right today. But one more afternoon, and the portrait should be done."

"Duncan will be glad to hear it," said Penny. "He is pleased with the progress so far."

He would likely also be pleased to have her out of his house, Emily thought with uncharacteristic self-pity.

Below in the foyer, the front door opened. A minute later, she heard Mr. McAllister's step on the stairs, just before he entered the room. It must have been windy outside; his hair was ruffled and his cheeks ruddy.

"Good afternoon, Lady Tuncliffe, Lord Rossley, Penny," he said, moving straight to his chaotic desk. He rooted through the scattered papers for a minute, finally withdrawing a sheaf of drawings and what appeared to be an account book. "If you will excuse me, I need to finish some work." Without another word, he exited the room. Moments later, the door to his tiny study at the back of the house clicked closed.

"Mr. McAllister is keeping to himself these days," Emily commented as she put the last paintbrush into her drawstring bag.

"I do not understand it," Penny mused. She nibbled her lower lip. "He has always done his work here, at his desk. But in the last week, I've nae seen him for more than five minutes at a stretch. I wonder whether he is trying to hide something from me."

"The other day, he sent round a note that he would not be able to meet me for our boxing session," Alex added. The two men had been sparring regularly at Jackson's.

"I doubt he has had time to go to Jackson's himself," Penny said. "He has been meeting with clients at all hours of the day and night. And when he is not out, he is in the study adding up figures. I wish I were more talented at mathematics, as I could be of some use to him. I am worried that he is working far too hard."

As Emily pondered Penny's words, she wished she could take back the words she had thrown at Mr. McAllister last week. Although she had been angry — in fact, she still was — she could have let him know in a more diplomatic way that she appreciated his efforts but did not want his help. It appeared that he had much more on his mind than their argument; it seemed cruel to add to his woes by carrying a grudge.

She needed to learn how to take control of her life without alienating those who wished her well, however misguided their actions.

Emily resolved to apologize for her churlishness. However, it was doubtful that she would have a chance to do so soon. Mr. McAllister obviously wished to avoid her, and it was difficult to say sorry to someone you never saw.

The following afternoon, Alex glanced around the sitting room, as though expecting a servant to materialize from behind a chair. When none appeared, he slid across the sofa until he was at Penny's side.

"Perhaps Libby did not hear Emily's summons," Penny murmured.

Emily had left the room to visit the necessary, and had rung for Libby to serve as chaperone.

"Whatever the reason, our opportunities to be alone are deuced rare," Alex replied, as he stroked the side of Penny's cheek. Quickly, before she could protest, he lowered his head and kissed her.

It was not the first kiss the couple had stolen, but each was as sweet as the last, Alexander thought. Penny's arms slid about his neck.

"Mmmm," she murmured. Then, slowly, she drew away. "While Emily is gone, there is something I must discuss with you."

"Are you sure you want to spend this time talking?"

Penny flushed. "Alex, be serious! I am very worried about Duncan. Something has gone dreadfully wrong between him and Emily, but he will not discuss it with me."

Alex nodded. For propriety's sake, he put a few inches back between them on the sofa. "I know. Em wanders out of the room every time I mention the subject."

"I suspect your sister is as stubborn — and as willfully blind — as my brother." Penny twisted a ginger curl around her finger. Alex tried to keep his eyes off the gesture and to focus on the problem at hand.

"I have given this a great deal of thought," he admitted. "It is more than obvious that each fosters a *tendre* for the other. The way Em used to smile each time McAllister entered the room made it obvious enough. And he certainly seemed to spend a great deal of time watching her work."

"Indeed, until last week I had never seen him at home so often during the day. I am certain it was not my sparkling conversation, nor Cook's seed cakes, that drew him here." She paused. "Whatever has come between them, it pains me to see it. Two people more deserving of happiness I have rarely met."

Alex cracked his knuckles.

"Must you do that?"

"Oh, sorry, I forgot you dislike it." He clasped his hands together in his lap. "I was just wondering whether we are making mountains out of molehills. Perhaps your brother has simply decided to focus more on his business."

Penny sighed. "He is probably driving himself because Father and Mother are due to arrive in London soon."

"What effect would that have on his work habits?" Alexander reached for his cup of tea and sipped.

"Father and Duncan have never seen eye to eye on his decision to become an architect. As Duncan is the oldest son, Father had always assumed that he would take over the family business. And while our brother Neil has always done admirably, Father still resents the fact that Duncan chose to go his own way."

"Fathers rarely enjoy that, believe me."

Penny smiled. She had heard a great deal about Alex's difficulties with his father. "Duncan has always been determined, not just to be an architect, but to be a wildly successful one. He could have stayed in Scotland, but he felt he had more scope for his ambitions here in London. He desperately wants to be the toast of the town — not for its own sake, but so that he can justify his choice of career to Father."

The couple lapsed into silence for a moment. Then a thought struck Alexander. "Your parents will be in Town within a few days?"

Penny nodded.

"I would like to meet them, if it is possible," he said, trying to sound casual.

"Why?"

"Why should I not? I am curious to meet the man who has driven McAllister to such heights of ambition." It was a weak parry, he knew, and the look in Penny's hazel eyes showed that she did not believe a word of it.

He definitely wanted to meet Penny's father. In private. But he was not quite ready to lay his entire hand on the table.

Not until he was positive how Penny would play hers.

As he heard Emily's footsteps in the corridor, he quickly launched into a story about an amusing man he had once encountered in Covent Garden. If Penny suspected the reason for his quick change of subject, she gave no indication.

Seven

Emily looked around the completed studio. The workers had left just twenty minutes before, and motes of plaster dust still hung in the air. There was not a stick of furniture in the room. And yet, it was the most beautiful chamber she had ever seen.

Light flooded in through enormous Palladian windows and reflected off the plain, creamy walls. The sunshine seemed to soar to the high ceiling, which was adorned with a clouded sky and rimmed by a pale blue molding.

As she walked around the perimeter, she felt like a woman in a dream. Finally, after years of wishing for a safe and quiet place to paint, she had a room that exceeded her wildest expectations.

Although she had supervised every other part of the renovations closely, she had only peeked into the studio a few times. She had been so afraid that it would not come close to the vision she had in her mind's eye. Telling herself that any studio would be a gift, she had resolved not to hope for too much.

But the room was delightful. Using an ingenious pulley system, she opened and closed a section of one window designed to ventilate the chamber while minimizing breezes that could blow her sketches about. Then she wandered across the room and ran a slippered toe over a frame in the floor that held a removable canvas drop cloth in place. She had not asked for such a convenience — had never even imagined it. Nor had she asked for the picture rail that ran about three sides of the room. It would be perfect for hanging her favorite canvases, far out of sight of most visitors to the house.

She was stroking an elegant, built-in shelf that had not been in the original plans when she heard a voice behind her. "It should be just the right size for your palette," Mr. McAllister said, coming into the room.

Emily had not even heard Gertie answer the front door. She turned, her mind bubbling with joy, surprise, embarrassment, and regret. "I do not know how to thank you, Mr. McAllister," she said. "This room surpasses anything I could have imagined. It is worth far more than Susannah's portrait."

"So you are happy?"

"Happy?" She grinned, spread her arms wide and spun around like a child. "I am ecstatic!"

"Music to an architect's ears."

"I am a most satisfied client. If ever you need a recommendation letter, I would be happy to write a glowing one."

An odd look crossed his face. He crossed to the wall of windows and looked out at the roses nodding in the late afternoon sunshine. "I may just take you up on that, if my clients would stop fleeing like livestock from a burning barn."

"Is business that bad?" Emily asked, reluctant to pry but wanting to help if she could.

With a start, Mr. McAllister turned from the window. "It has been better," he said, shaking his head. "But I did not come here to talk about that. I wanted to thank you in person for the portrait of Susannah. You have captured much more than just her hair and eyes. I believe you have captured a slip of her soul as well."

A warm rush of pride surged through Emily. She had been satisfied with the portrait, but she was too close to her work to judge it objectively. "I am glad you like it."

"I plan to hang it over the fireplace in the sitting room this very evening."

Over the fireplace? Where everyone could see it? She opened her mouth to protest, and then clamped it shut. Where on earth had she expected him to hang it? He had worked long hours to compensate her for her work. He could hardly be expected to display the portrait in the cellar.

"Mr. McAllister —" Emily began, just as he said, "Lady Tuncliffe —"

They laughed.

"Please, speak first," Mr. McAllister said, crossing the room, then leaning against the tiled mantelpiece. As always, she admired his animal grace.

"I wish to apologize for my angry words the other day," she began. "I realize now that you were only trying to be helpful, and that I responded with rudeness. After years of bowing to the commands of others, I suppose I have become rather childish about getting my own way."

"Don't be so harsh on yourself," Mr. McAllister cut in. "I have a terrible tendency to believe that my view on any topic is the only correct one. Just ask Penny." A rueful smile creased his features, and her heart jumped into an odd rhythm.

"I think your interest in the affairs of others is admirable. It is not a fault of which you should be ashamed."

"It is just that I seem to have been pushing against strong wills all my life, from my father to my clients," he said, running a hand absently through his hair. "I suppose I have become used to jousting at windmills."

"You see me as strong-willed?"

"Who could not?" He quirked an eyebrow at her. "It is not every young woman who could take on the management of a major residential renovation. Or teach herself to paint over the objections of others."

Because he had known Simon, he had guessed at the misery of her life in Hampshire. Once again, Emily longed to explain what it had been like.

Obey him, and serve him, love, honor, and keep him. The words of her marriage vows echoed through her mind, unbidden. She had promised before God and her family to honor her husband. And although Simon had broken his vows from almost the moment he had spoken them, she would not do the same.

"I am certain I am not the first artist to paint in secret," she said lightly.

"If ever you change your mind about the secrecy . . ." He glanced out the window at the tiny garden.

"Yes, Mr. McAllister?" The tattoo of her

heart increased, but it was no longer a pleasant sensation.

"I am reluctant to broach this issue, but I feel it is my duty to do so. You should have the opportunity to consider it." He stopped.

"Please continue, Mr. McAllister. I promise, I will not bite you."

"You may be feeling hungrier than you realize." He sighed. "I encountered Lady Farnham in Oxford Street the other day. She had heard of Susannah's portrait and wanted to see it. So, naturally, I invited her to my home for a viewing."

A flicker of dread sparked in Emily's chest.

"She was intrigued by your work, and wondered whether you might be interested in painting a portrait of her daughters. I tried to dissuade her, but she was insistent. Now, I know what you have said before —"

"No," Emily interrupted. "I have said no before, and I will say no again."

"But you have not heard her proposal."

"If it involves me painting another portrait, that is all I need to hear." She struggled to keep her voice quiet, to keep this discussion calm and controlled. "I thank you for bringing her offer to my attention — truly, I appreciate your efforts — but I

126

do not wish to paint professionally."

"The sum she is prepared to pay is substantial."

"It does not matter."

He pursed his lips and puffed out his breath. "Lady Tuncliffe, I believe you are being too hasty. Dinnae you think you should consider any commissions carefully before dismissing them?"

Why would he not leave her alone? Why was he pushing her into anger?

"How often must I say this, Mr. McAllister? I paint simply to amuse myself."

He flushed a dull red. "And how often must I say in response that it is a sinful waste of your God-given gifts to hide them away?"

"They are my gifts, and I will use them as I choose." She felt like an actress, condemned to repeat the same lines night after night on some bewitched stage.

"And if you choose to throw them away, daubing at canvases to hide in a cellar, I am to sit idly by and say nothing?" He pushed himself away from the mantel and paced in front of the windows. The sunlight glinted in his hair like new pennies. "Ach, you have a prodigious talent, and someone eager to help you use it. It is an opportunity such as I lie awake dreaming of — and yet you throw it away! You keep telling me you want to be independent."

"I do want to be independent!"

"And yet you will not grasp an opportunity that falls into your lap!"

"I do not need to earn a living." Emily's voice seemed to scratch her throat. "I have a widow's portion. My husband did not leave me destitute."

"Painting could give you the stature and the income to live life as a true Original." His eyes were alight with an inner fire she could not understand. "Your future would be secure. But you are too afraid to take the chance."

"That is enough!" Emily thought she had been angry before, during their disagreement about Charles Walsh. But the emotion she had felt that day paled before the fury she felt now.

"You are just like Simon, always telling me what to do, where to go, what to think. He was always telling me I was not good enough — or depraved enough, to be more precise — for his tastes. I was married to him, and so I had to listen, but I owe you no vow of obedience! I will thank you to be silent on this issue."

Mr. McAllister gave a short bark of

laughter. "Is that why you will never say a word against Simon? Because you promised obedience?"

"I will never say a word against Simon because he was my husband! Because I vowed before God and before my family that I would honor him." Emily clenched her hands together to keep them from trembling.

To her horror, she felt tears welling. How had her intention to apologize to Mr. McAllister gone so far astray?

He crossed the room and stood before her. To her utter consternation, he rested his hands on her shoulders.

They warmed her as no hearth ever had.

Mortified at the bolt of attraction surging through her, she lowered her gaze. Her anger began shattering into tiny, harmless shards.

"Simon is dead," he murmured. "The vow, as I recall, extends only 'so long as ye both shall live.'"

She shook her head. She could not start to think that way, or everything would come undone.

Mr. McAllister put a hand under her chin and tilted her head toward him. "Tell me. I shan't tell a soul."

She shook her head again. Her mind

could comprehend little outside the barrage of sensations his closeness called forth. Gooseflesh danced along her arms and the hairs at the bottom of her chignon.

"I knew Simon. You cannae reduce him in my estimation. He made my life a living hell at Harrow, and I haven't met a man since who was less worthy of regard, let alone protection." He paused and stroked the side of her cheek. "What did he do to you?"

Emily closed her eyes. She could not remember the last time another human being had touched her with such tenderness.

"Tell me," he urged, his voice soft. "Just whatever you need to say. You will feel better. I promise."

The temptation was too great.

"I hated Simon," she whispered.

She did not feel better. She felt worse. How could a woman hate her own husband? And how would Mr. McAllister, of all people — a man who had obviously adored his late wife — understand such an emotion?

"I hated him, too," he said, his voice like a lullaby. "Tell me why you did."

Emily knew she should move away from him, but she could not. "It started about two months after we were married," she began. "Until then, he had tried to behave as any husband would. We had our meals together. He worked on the estate. We shared few interests, and I felt no warmth for him, but it seemed that we might have a marriage no worse than many others. I hoped it would be built on respect, if not on love."

She stopped, took a deep breath.

"Then he disappeared for a week. He left no note, no indication of where he had gone or when he would be back. I was frantic. I went to see the local squire, but when I told him my story, he laughed. He informed me that Simon was wont to go missing for weeks at a time. His erratic behavior was legendary throughout Hampshire. I had no idea."

Mr. McAllister squeezed her shoulder. "It must have been terrible."

His touch gave her courage to continue. "He did finally come back, eight days after he left. It was very late at night, and I was asleep. I heard a terrible racket in the entryway. Before I could summon the butler to find out what was happening, I heard Simon shouting my name."

Seven years later, the memory still nauseated her.

"I pulled on my wrapper and ran to the top of the stairs. To my embarrassment, Simon was accompanied by three friends. They were covered in dirt, as though they had been in a fight. They . . . they had two women with them."

Mr. McAllister swore under his breath.

"He shouted at me to be useful, to bring some food and some bottles of claret we had in the cellar. And to hurry up, or he would make me sorry."

Emily drew a shaky breath. "I had always sensed he had a vicious streak, but I had never seen proof of it. That night, I had all the evidence I needed."

She stopped. She had told no one this story, ever. Not even Clare.

"Tell me." Mr. McAllister's taut voice penetrated behind her closed lids. He gripped her shoulder. "Did he hurt you?"

Her eyes flew open. "Not physically, no."

His hold on her relaxed. "Well, that is a small mercy. But I am sure he did much else. If he were not already in his grave, I would call him out myself."

It was Mr. McAllister's vow of support that did her in. Suddenly, the words tumbled out. She told him how Simon's friends had stayed for three days, during which the men had leered at her and the women had mocked her clothing and manners, while Simon laughed.

There were many other memories. The times she would discover the housekeeping money gone, and would know that Simon had taken it to wager on cards in the gaming hells of Portsmouth. The way he had harangued the staff. The year of their first — and only — Christmas party, when he had become so intoxicated on punch that he had called the local magistrate's wife an unrepeatable name, making himself — and, by proxy, Emily — a local pariah.

The stories streamed out, year after year of pain and embarrassment. It was only when she remembered the day a few weeks before he died, when Simon had called her a useless baggage who could not even perform the services of a brood mare and deliver him a child, that she had the will to stop her voice.

She could not tell Mr. McAllister that. Of all the memories, that one still hurt too much.

Mr. McAllister had remained quiet throughout her litany, simply encouraging her softly when her voice failed.

Hot tears were streaming down her face. He handed her a clean linen handkerchief.

"I hated him," she whispered. "When he fell off his horse in a drunken stupor, I was glad. That is my secret. My husband broke his neck, and the only thing I felt was blessed relief. I will burn in hell, but I cannot help myself."

Mr. McAllister still held her by both shoulders. "You will not burn in hell, if God is at all merciful," he said, drawing her into his arms.

She knew she should resist, but it felt so good to lean against him. She could feel his heart beating softly through the thin muslin of her pale yellow day dress.

"God would not be so cruel as to make you keep company with Simon for all eternity," he added.

At his bleak joke, she smiled. "That is a terrible thing to say."

"Believe me, it is the most polite thing I can think of to say under the circumstances." He pulled away from her, and once again tilted up her chin. "And you have told no one of this, all these years?"

"Clare knows some of it. So does Alex. And I think Lucy suspects a little. But most of it, no."

"You are very brave, and a much better person than Simon Wallace deserved."

"No," she whispered, thinking about the

heir she had been unable to give her husband.

"Yes," Mr. McAllister said firmly. And then, to her shock, he bent his head and kissed her.

She forgot everything — Simon, the arguments about her painting — as Mr. McAllister's lips touched hers. His kiss was at once more gentle and more intimate than Simon's had ever been. It was as though she stood before him unclad and defenseless.

As he deepened the kiss, she realized she did not want to defend herself against it. Instead, she raised herself on the tips of her toes and twined her hands about his neck. She ran her fingers through the curly ginger hair at his nape.

He moved his hands from her shoulders to her waist and drew her against him. She felt the restrained strength in his touch, and yet she was not afraid. Rather, she was eager, curious, and comforted beyond measure. She pressed against his solid chest, and he groaned, deep in his throat, and pulled away.

"You are one of the only good things in my life right now," he said, touching her cheek. Then he trailed a finger to her chin, and along the column of her throat. She was lost in the long dormant sensations he was calling forth.

When his finger touched the lace of her neckline, her breath caught in her throat.

This had to stop.

She could not let Mr. McAllister think she was a woman worth courting.

For she was nothing of the kind.

"Mr. McAllister," she whispered, calling on every reserve of strength she possessed. "Mr. McAllister," she said more loudly. "I cannot. It is not right."

He loosened his hold on her but did not move away. "Do you not enjoy it?" His voice was questioning and teasing, hopeful and soft.

Emily could not lie. She didn't want him to stop, but she had to explain. She had to tell him how she had failed her husband by failing to conceive a child.

How on earth could she begin?

Her stomach roiled as shame engulfed her.

"I do enjoy it," she mumbled. "Believe me, I do. But Simon . . ."

She paused, trying to find the courage to repeat the names that Simon had called her, the epithets he had had every right to throw.

But Mr. McAllister had already dropped

his hands to his sides.

"You feel it is too soon after your husband's death?" he asked, his face unreadable.

Her shoulders sagged. This explanation would satisfy him. She could walk away with some semblance of her dignity and privacy intact.

Emily took the easy way out. She nodded.

"Yes. People would talk." That was true enough.

One day, when she had scraped up the courage, she would be completely honest.

"And appearances are that important to you?" His voice was brittle.

She nodded again, then looked away, around the room he had so thoughtfully designed for her. Her throat constricted as she thought of how kind he had been to her, and how hard it was to hurt him this way.

But it had to be done. She could not encourage his suit.

"One day, Lady Tuncliffe, I hope you learn to stop hiding behind propriety and to be honest about what you want. If you should ever care to tell me the true reasons behind your reluctance, I would be curious to hear them."

A silence fell on them. There did not seem to be anything left to say — nothing, at least, that Emily was brave enough to utter.

After what seemed like hours, Mr. McAllister moved toward the door. "As the renovations and the portrait are both complete, I suppose this is good-bye, Lady Tuncliffe. Thank you again for hiring me. I have enjoyed working with you." With a stiff bow, he walked away.

She could not stand his disappointment.

"Mr. McAllister, wait!"

He turned, and crossed his arms in front of his chest. His face was devoid of expression.

She had to do something to make up for her behavior. But what?

Suddenly, it came to her.

"I cannot throw propriety to the winds all at once. But perhaps you are right, and I was too quick to dismiss Lady Farnham's offer." She willed her heart to stop racing. "I will meet with Lady Farnham to at least discuss her commission."

He smiled briefly. "That is a small victory."

"It is all I can do."

"I will ask Lady Farnham to approach you directly. I assume you will not need me to perform the introduction?"

The thought of seeing Mr. McAllister again made Emily shake with dread. "No."

"Thank you, Lady Tuncliffe." This time, when he turned to leave, she did not stop him.

His footsteps echoed along the corridor. The front door opened and closed.

She slumped against the cream-colored wall. It had been necessary to wound his male pride, to cut off the tenderness between them before it could grow into anything else.

She suspected that she had already waited too long, at least in her own case. What she felt for Duncan McAllister had already grown beyond mere friendship and attraction. She had just been too willfully blind to see it.

But an attachment would be dangerous. It had already led her to do the one thing she had sworn not to do: consider another painting commission.

That was how things happened with men: once they were close to you, they manipulated you for their own ends. And even if they had the best of intentions, the fact remained that the closer a woman became to a man, the less control she had over her life.

Emily was not willing to relinquish her independence so soon. Even if she had been able to have children, she would be a fool to marry again.

She dabbed her streaming eyes with the handkerchief he had given her. It smelled of sandalwood and clean wool, evoking the feeling of his arms about her.

She had blocked memories from her mind before. It would just be a matter of will to do so again, she told herself as she moved to the window to stare unseeingly at the garden.

Eight

Thank heaven for Lucy, Emily thought as she listened to her youngest sister's boisterous chatter. Without her, Emily would have been much more likely to obsess about her distressing encounter in the studio with Mr. McAllister the previous afternoon. But she barely had time for a thought of her own; Lucy was full of news about the gentlemen she had met during her season.

"Mr. Wilson is entertaining, even though he has a terrible stammer. I think that is something one could get used to in time, don't you, Em?"

"I suppose one can get used to anything if one puts one's mind to it. If he is kind and entertaining, I doubt a speech impediment would matter." Emily's eye was drawn to a fly cavorting in one of the sunbeams illuminating her salon.

"But then there is also Lord Rothmere. He wishes to take me for a carriage ride in Hyde Park tomorrow. He is rather dull, and I would prefer to ride than to travel by carriage. But Papa says I should consider all invitations."

"Papa has always spoken thus. In his view, any gentleman is a good gentleman." Emily kept her voice neutral, even as her mind flew back to the days of her own season. She had not liked Simon Wallace one bit the evening they were introduced at her coming-out ball.

"What could possibly displease you?" her father had teased her the following morning. "He is rich, he is titled, and he cuts a fine figure on the dance floor."

"There is something hard about him, Papa," Emily had murmured. "I do not like the look in his eyes."

"Don't be mulish, Emily. Give him a chance. He has already sent around his card. I believe he is smitten."

Within six months, she and Simon had married. It was only after they had moved to Hampshire that she had learned how true her initial impressions had been.

To Lucy, she said now, "Follow your heart and don't allow Papa to force you into a liaison you don't want. If he becomes unreasonable, you may always come to live with me."

"Oh, that would be lovely!" Lucy exclaimed. "You and Alex and I could have the grandest times!"

"What times are these that you are planning, Lucy?" Alex asked, strolling into the room. "If there is a picnic or an excursion to the theater in the works, I will be there in my finest."

"Lucy was just speculating on how we could entertain ourselves if she took up residence here as well."

"It would be just like old times," Alex said, sinking into a damask-covered wing chair, Emily's latest acquisition. "Although such an arrangement may not last forever." His eyes were glittering with amusement.

"What are you hiding, Alex?" Lucy asked. "You look like the cat who has swallowed the canary — and a few dozen other birds, as well."

Alex grinned. "I am glad you are both here, as I have some momentous news to share."

Emily and Lucy both leaned forward.

"Have you won a fortune at cards?" Lucy breathed. "Or killed a man in a duel?"

"Don't be ridiculous," Emily chided her sister, laughing. "Would he look so pleased with himself if he had just left a man bleeding in some isolated meadow?"

"Well, if he were a very nasty man —" Lucy began.

"If you will be quiet a minute, I will tell

you," Alex cut in, ruffling his little sister's newly upswept hair.

"Alex! My ringlets!"

"My apologies. I should have been more careful." He paused, then stood up and threw open his arms dramatically. "I have offered for Miss McAllister, and she has consented to become my wife!"

Joy surged through Emily. She could think of no better match for her brother than the kind and gentle Scotswoman.

"I am so happy for you, Alex!" she cried, rushing across the room to throw her arms about her brother's neck. On the other side of him, Lucy had encircled his waist and was hugging him with equal vigor.

"It is not cast in stone yet, however," he said, when his two sisters had detached themselves and returned to their seats. "Penny has asked for time to find a new housekeeper for her brother, and I have agreed. A cousin from Perthshire may be able to come to London. Penny, bless her, refuses to move until she can ensure that Duncan will not be abandoned."

Emily's heart contracted as she thought how much the architect would miss his sister's company in the small house in Chelsea. And yet, she knew he would genuinely wish Penny and Alex well.

"I have also not yet had the opportunity to ask her father's permission, so this news must remain a secret between us for the moment." He gave Lucy a stern glance. "That means you must tell no one — not even Papa."

Lucy drew herself up straight and gave him her haughtiest stare. "Of course, you can trust me to keep a secret," she said. "I am not a child anymore."

"I know that, Lucy," he said affectionately. "And, with luck, I will not ask you to keep it long. Miss McAllister's parents are arriving in London soon for an extended visit. I hope to discuss this matter with her father next Tuesday evening. Penny has invited you and me to dinner, Em."

"As usual, I will miss all the fun!" Lucy wailed. "Even if I had been invited to the McAllisters', I could not go — I have already accepted a dinner invitation from some dull friends of Papa's for that evening, and he would be upset if I declined."

Emily only half heard Lucy's protest, as the sound of her own heartbeat thundered in her ears. To see Mr. McAllister again so soon! She had hoped to take a few weeks to compose herself so that the next time they met they would be able to treat each other as friends.

"You will have your turn, Lucy," Alex consoled his sister. "If Penny's father approves my suit, there will be many other joint celebrations."

Emily's heart fell to the bottom of her slippers. He was right. If the betrothal came to pass, the Denham and McAllister families would likely socialize often before the wedding.

"Are you certain you want me there next Tuesday night?" Emily asked her brother. "It is such a personal time, after all."

"Em, I need you there to give me courage as I go in, and to prop up my spirits if all does not go as planned!"

Emily felt childish. She could not abandon Alex if he wanted her to accompany him. She would just have to learn to deal with Duncan McAllister sooner rather than later.

"I would be honored to be there, Alex," she said, squeezing her brother's hand. "And once the elder Mr. McAllister agrees — as I am certain he will, if he has a modicum of sense — I would like to host a betrothal party for you and Penny."

In for a penny, in for a pound.

Lucy clapped her hands. "A wonderful idea! That will give you a chance to display this fine new house, and it will give me an

146

opportunity to meet the mysterious Mr. McAllister and his parents." Lucy had gone to Vauxhall one evening with Penny, Alex, and Emily, but Mr. McAllister had been too busy with work to accompany them.

"I would like the party to be in your honor as well, Lucy. I had hoped to host one as soon as the house was completed."

"You may not have time to host any parties," Alex informed Emily. "It appears that your portrait of Susannah is causing quite the sensation among the Piers Sherrington set."

"Piers Sherrington!" Lucy exclaimed, wincing. "Where on earth did you run into Lord Snivel?"

Alex hooted with laughter. "Lord *Snivel?*"

"Lucy, please," Emily said, restraining a giggle herself. "You are well past using such infantile expressions."

"Well, I suppose I am, but do you not think it suitable? It was either Lord Snivel or Sir Mighty-Dandy. Lord Snivel was shorter."

Alex nodded, covering his mouth.

"I must say, I was immensely relieved when he cried off his pursuit of Clarissa," Lucy concluded. "Pompous man!"

"Sherrington may be pompous, but he

has been generous in his praise of Em's painting. As have many others."

"Who else has seen it?" Emily's voice was sharp.

Oblivious to the edge in his sister's tone, Alex barreled forward. "This afternoon, Lady Farnham came back for what I gather was a second look. Duncan was out, but she said he had written her a note, telling her that you were willing to consider painting a picture of her daughters."

Alex fixed her with a mocking glare. "You did not tell me about her proposal. That is excellent news!"

"I am not sure I agree."

"Well, you should be quick to make up your mind, because I have the feeling that even more offers will soon be coming your way. Lady Farnham mentioned that she had told numerous friends about your picture. I would not be surprised if you were deluged with commissions to paint every child in the *ton*."

Emily could not share her brother's optimism. In fact, she could have wept with frustration. Not only was she the widow of one of the most outrageous drunkards in England, now she had also been exposed as an artist! Lady Farnham might as well have told the world that Emily was a courtesan.

"It looks as though you are about to become famous, Em," Alex said. "And with all these commissions, you will never want for funds."

"I may not accept any of those commissions — even Lady Farnham's," Emily said crisply.

"Why not, Emily?" Lucy asked. "You enjoyed painting the portrait of Susannah McAllister."

Yes, Emily thought, but the enjoyment she had derived from the experience had not come solely from the satisfaction of capturing the little girl on canvas. It had something more to do with the slight hint of a Scottish burr, afternoons of easy laughter, and the frisson of excitement that had swept through her whenever Mr. McAllister had leaned over her shoulder to observe her work.

She could share none of this with her siblings, however. Look where her romantic notions had led her already — into another man's arms, when she was barely out of mourning.

If Simon's past and her paintings had not already put her beyond the pale among the *ton*, an affair with a man so soon after Simon's death would certainly cause enough talk to make her an outcast forever.

She had to take control of her life. Right now.

"I cannot become a professional artist," Emily said in response to her sister's question.

"I know you think it is important to be proper. But why?" Lucy asked. "You are not like me, having to protect your reputation at every turn. As a widow, you can do anything you like!"

"It is not that simple," Emily replied, leaning back in her chair. She felt the beginnings of a headache drumming at her temples. "The *ton* has its rules, and I have always abided by them. I do not plan to stop now."

After all, she told herself, if society's dictates were so easy to flout, she could have fled Tuncliffe Manor, and Simon, years ago. But she had not, because that was not what was done.

Duncan was relieved that neither Lord Rossley nor any of his other acquaintances were at Gentleman Jackson's rooms this afternoon. In his present frame of mind, he was much safer practicing his pugilistic skills on a defenseless punching bag.

Besides, he had no energy left for conversation. He needed time to think.

Had he been wrong to kiss Lady Tuncliffe yesterday? At the time, it had seemed the most natural thing in the world.

Thwap! His hand connected satisfactorily with the leather bag.

He had lain awake most of the night trying to discern the reason behind her withdrawal from him, developing and discarding theories the way he sketched architectural designs until he found the one most suitable to a client's site, tastes, and budget.

He knew Lady Tuncliffe was not holding back because she found him unattractive. He was not a vain man, but he was an honest one, and he had seen desire in her eyes.

Given her hatred for Simon Wallace, he doubted that her late husband's death was the obstacle that stood between them.

He had considered the situation from every angle, and always came back to the same conclusion: she was reluctant to encourage a man who could not secure steady work.

It was the logical conclusion. What woman of sense would not be reluctant?

Thwap!

If his business continued along its current course, within a month he would have no commissions at all. Within a year, he would be a bankrupt.

When Lady Farnham had been the first to pull out of a commission, six months ago, he had been disappointed but not worried. Such things happened to all architects occasionally; it was part of the business.

But then other clients had begun sending in their regrets. The reasons they gave him varied. They had decided to postpone the project, or they had realized their funds were insufficient, or another architect — whom they refused to name — had devised a more pleasing design. Several had intimated that they did not trust his work, even though he had offered to provide sterling references. Few would give him the courtesy of withdrawing their offer in person; most of the refusals had come via letter. His desk was littered with them.

Charles Walsh informing him earlier today that his services would not be required to design the new wing of Walsh House had been the final straw.

The only client who had actually signed a contract in the last month had been Piers Sherrington. Thank heaven Duncan had secured that commitment before his friend had had a chance to reconsider.

Thwap! Duncan's hand was rapidly growing raw inside the cracked leather practice glove.

And then, of course, his parents were due to arrive any day. Why had they not visited six months ago, when he could have boasted to his father about his undeniable success?

Thwap! The pain of the left hook recoiled up Duncan's arm.

There was still some reason for optimism, however. Perhaps the renovation of Lady Tuncliffe's town house would be the turning point for his business.

Why could he not stop thinking about Lady Tuncliffe?

Against his will, his mind returned to their embrace in her studio. He remembered how she had felt against him, soft and warm and yielding. How hard it had been to release her, even when she had given him a patently false excuse for her coolness.

Thwap! He pounded the punching bag one last time and reeled away in exhaustion.

Perhaps Lady Tuncliffe's reluctance was all to the good. She was damnably determined to have her own way, and if they were ever to form an attachment, they might well spend all their time debating the merits of every notion she took into her head.

But such patterns could be broken, if the will to do so existed, he told himself as he stripped off his gloves and wiped the sweat from his brow with a small, threadbare towel.

He could not shake the notion that Lady Tuncliffe would be a pleasing life companion. They enjoyed each other's company, and he suspected that they would enjoy other things as well. Despite himself, he smiled.

All he needed to do was overcome her resistance to his suit. Solving his business woes should do the trick. In the meantime, though, a gentlemanly approach might be just the plaster to smooth over the cracks that had sprung up between them. It would be satisfying to pay court to Lady Tuncliffe; Duncan suspected that she had known little of compliments and kindness from Simon Wallace.

Pleased with his plan, he retrieved his jacket from a hook on the wall and left the boxing academy. There was no time like the present to solicit new commissions.

Nine

"I am so pleased you changed your mind and accepted my proposal," Lady Farnham bubbled. "I cannot tell you how enchanting I found your portrait of Susannah McAllister."

"Thank you," Emily murmured. With time, she was learning to accept praise for her work with good grace.

Some things took more adjustment. She was still a bit shocked to find herself standing before her easel in a disused bedroom in Lady Farnham's town house. Everything had happened so quickly. Yesterday she and Lady Farnham had met for tea, and the older woman had been persuasive. She had dismissed Emily's every protest with a wave of her heavily jeweled hand and had offered a sum — in advance — that would pay the salaries of Emily's small staff for the better part of a year.

It had seemed childish to refuse.

By the window in the bedroom sat Lady Farnham's daughters: fifteen-year-old Lady Pamela and seventeen-year-old Lady

Harriet. The girls were so unalike one would scarcely guess they were sisters. Pamela was dark, quiet, and thoughtful, while Harriet was fair, ebullient, and — not to be unkind — something of a bufflehead.

"Is this gown suitable, Lady Tuncliffe?" Harriet called out. "I thought it more flattering than the pink one."

"It will do very nicely," Emily said, trying to sound encouraging. Her charge's current pistachio colored gown was the eighth dress Lady Harriet had donned in the space of an hour. The girl had rejected the seven previous options for a variety of reasons: too revealing, too demure, too showy, too dull.

Emily hoped this dress would finally please Lady Harriet, so that the girl would sit long enough for Emily to produce some preliminary sketches.

"You are very patient with them," Lady Farnham observed.

"You forget, my first commission was a rambunctious three-year-old. I am already a battle veteran." Emily smiled as she remembered how much she had enjoyed her sessions with the sunny-tempered child.

Susannah took after her father in many ways. But Mr. McAllister's demeanor during their last encounter had been anything but sunny. With a slight shiver, Emily remembered the look in his eyes as he had turned to leave.

However, one good thing had come out of that disastrous afternoon: her decision to consider Lady Farnham's commission.

Mr. McAllister had been absolutely correct, Emily admitted as she began recording some quick pencil impressions of her young subjects. Yes, he might have been trying to force her to do things his way, but he had had a point.

Surviving on her widow's portion would be possible, but such a life would involve doing without, to some degree. And there would always be the chance that she could fall back into dependence on others.

To be truly independent, she had to have another income. And, as Mr. McAllister had said, she had the unique good fortune to have a talent she could exploit.

She devoutly wished it had been something more respectable. But if it was a choice between respectable penury and somewhat scandalous security, she had finally admitted that the latter was preferable.

"How did you become interested in oil painting?" Lady Pamela asked. Her face was devoid of scorn.

"Yes, I am also curious," said Lady Farnham. "I learned the basics of watercolors, of course, but I always found that art insipid. However, painting in oils had never occurred to me."

"A teacher taught me the basics of color, and I began mixing my own paints using some materials I found in the attic at my late husband's country estate," Emily began. "Lord Tuncliffe traveled frequently and I sought amusement. I had never been overly fond of watercolors, either, but I enjoyed the bold colors and the textures offered by oils. I used the rudiments of drawing and watercolor, along with several rather gloomy ancestral portraits at Tuncliffe Manor, to teach myself. But I by no means consider myself a skilled artist. Someone such as Charles Walsh, who has had formal instruction and has visited the great galleries on the Continent, is in a completely different sphere."

"Skill can be honed by instruction, but talent is inherent," Lady Farnham said. "Do not denigrate yourself simply because you cannot join the gentlemen's club of the Royal Academy. If I did not think you skilled, I would not have hired you."

As they continued to chat, Emily realized with growing amazement that neither Lady Farnham nor her daughters considered her an outcast for her work. Then again, Lady Farnham was a known iconoclast. She had been one of the first to challenge the supremacy of the patronesses of Almack's, by waltzing with her husband in its assembly rooms when most people in England had barely heard of the scandalous dance.

Much as Emily was enjoying this session with Lady Farnham and her daughters, she keenly felt Mr. McAllister's absence. This was the first time she had painted for others when there was no chance that she would hear his voice in the corridor, that he would wander into the room to play a foolish prank on Susannah, or that he would stand at Emily's back to observe her work.

It was just as well.

"How do you happen to know Mr. McAllister?" she heard herself asking Lady Farnham.

What was wrong with her? Why couldn't she stop thinking about the man?

"I had asked him to draw up some plans for a small addition to the back of this house."

"He does wonderful work, does he not?"

Emily asked. "He renovated my town house, and I was most pleased with the results."

Uncharacteristically, her companion fell silent.

Emily looked up from her easel.

"What is the matter, Lady Farnham?"

"Well, my dear, I hate to be the bearer of bad tidings. But if I were you, I would carefully inspect the work of Mr. McAllister and his contractors."

"For what reason?"

Lady Farnham lowered her voice. "I have it on very good authority that Mr. McAllister cuts corners on his designs."

For a moment, Emily was too stunned to speak. Finally, she sputtered, "I can think of nothing that could be further from the truth! In fact, when we were collaborating on the plans for my renovation, he suggested several modifications that increased the cost but which, he assured me, would also substantially improve the finished product."

Lady Farnham smiled. "I am glad to hear that your project went well, Lady Tuncliffe. For truly, I like Mr. McAllister, and I do not wish him ill. But when I heard about the collapse of that conservatory, I was shocked."

"A collapse!" Emily could not believe that Mr. McAllister could be responsible for such a calamity.

"Why, yes. It was on the country estate of Lord Langdon! Can you imagine? I do not know the man personally, but I'm certain he must have been furious."

Emily, confused but determined to understand, cut her off. "I do know the man personally. As a matter of fact, he is my brother-in-law. He and my sister recommended Mr. McAllister to me in glowing terms."

Lady Farnham gaped at Emily.

"And I can assure you, Lady Farnham, that their conservatory has not collapsed, nor has ever been in danger of doing so. Why, I just received a letter from my sister two days ago, in which she said how much she enjoyed sitting in the new addition on sunny afternoons!"

Lady Farnham stared at her. "My goodness! However can such a rumor have begun?"

"I have no idea. Where did you hear it first?"

"Why, from Sarah Nelson, I believe. I do not know where she heard it. But I did verify the story with several friends. They all reported hearing a similar tale — although the stories did vary. One person said she had heard that it was a country squire's portico in Somerset that fell down, while another thought it was a barrister's kitchen in Warwickshire. It was always somewhere in the country." Lady Farnham sat down heavily on a small Sheraton chair, her face pale. "I cannot believe I was so foolish as to believe the story I was told without checking with Lord Langdon directly. To think of the harm I may have unwittingly done to Mr. McAllister's reputation! For I have shared the tale with several others since."

"Do not berate yourself, Lady Farnham. If many people had heard similar stories, you cannot be faulted as their sole source."

"I even heard one of the fabrications from another architect I asked to bid on the commission, Nigel Harris. As soon as he heard Mr. McAllister's name, he was quite eager to inform me that he had heard similar things."

Nigel Harris. Why did that name sound so familiar? And why had he been so eager to repeat a slanderous tale of a fellow architect?

"Did you award the commission to Mr. Harris in the end?"

"No, I did not, now that you ask. In fact,

I have postponed the project, until I can find the right architect. I did not care for the designs Mr. Harris prepared — I found them rather old-fashioned and dull."

"Is he an older man, then?"

"No, he is probably of an age with Mr. McAllister."

Nigel Harris. Perhaps he was some family acquaintance — the son of one of her father's cronies, or a neighbor of her mother.

Suddenly, Emily remembered where she had heard the name. Simon had mumbled it once, on returning from one of his disappearances.

"Harris should be shot," she recalled him muttering as he sat at the dining room table at Tuncliffe Manor, drinking endless cups of weak tea and shouting at Cook to bring him a cold cloth.

"Who is Harris?" Emily had inquired, more out of an innate tendency to make conversation than out of any real desire to know.

"Nigel Harris. Old boy. Harrow. Used to be great chums, but hadn't seen him in months. Met up with him in Town, two days ago." Simon had rubbed his temples. "Took me to some gaming hell he knew. Got me into my cups, then practically won the shirt off my back. Lucky I had a horse to ride home on."

One of Simon's louche acquaintances. If he was anything like Simon, he would think nothing of ruining one man's reputation to further his own.

Could this be the reason why Mr. McAllister's business had suddenly evaporated?

Trying to keep the cold fury flooding her veins from icing her voice, Emily asked, "Would you remember, Lady Farnham, where Mr. Harris has his office?"

Emily glanced around the small chamber. It was dark and rather dusty. The burgundy velvet curtains at the window were inexpertly patched.

Altogether, not a setting to inspire confidence.

A dour housemaid had ushered her into this room at the back of a house on the unfashionable side of Clerkenwell. "Mr. Harris is out, ma'am, but we're expectin' him back any minute," she had said before shuffling away.

And so Emily sat, with not a cup of tea to comfort her, as she nervously waited for the architect to appear.

Perhaps Lady Farnham's word was good enough proof, Emily thought. She could just get up and walk out the door and . . .

No, she told herself. Hearsay and rumor were at the root of this whole debacle. She would hear the lies from the horse's mouth before she would proceed further.

After several minutes, he strolled into the room. He was of average height, with thinning, sandy hair and pale gray eyes. With his gray coat and faded neckcloth, he seemed almost a wraith — and much older than his years, if he was indeed the man who had been Simon's schoolmate.

"Good afternoon, Mrs. Lewis, is it?"

"Yes, that's right." Emily had decided a false name would be best, as Mr. Harris could easily connect her real name to Simon, and possibly to Lord Langdon.

"What can I do for you, Mrs. Lewis? I do not usually meet clients without an appointment."

"I am sorry to have arrived uninvited, but you came so highly recommended, and I happened to be passing right by your house."

"Well, that was convenient." He sat down at the scarred oak desk, folded his hands on the surface, and waited.

Emily took a deep breath. "I am looking to make some renovations to my town house," she began, hoping that God would not strike her down as she began to spin a web of half-truths and prevarications. "My late husband had so wanted to bring the house up to date, and I am determined that the work will be done in his honor."

"That is very thoughtful of you. Where is your home?"

"In Mayfair." She had almost told him Berkeley Square, but that was a little too close to the facts.

He leaned forward. "An eminent address."

She tried not to flinch away. "Yes. That is why I want the house to be in the first stare of fashion." Briefly, she outlined the changes she supposedly wanted made — the alterations, in fact, that Mr. McAllister had done.

"That is quite a substantial list, Mrs. Lewis. A house that needs that much work may not be worth saving."

"I am sentimentally attached to it. I would like to try." She was quickly concluding why Mr. Harris had had to resort to subterfuge to win clients.

"Very well," he said, pulling a sheaf of foolscap from a desk drawer. "I will do my best. What budget did you have in mind?"

She named a sum — the exact fee Duncan had charged.

The architect snorted.

"I am sorry, Mrs. Lewis. I sincerely doubt that the scope of the work you envision could be done for even twice that amount."

This was the moment when Emily had to play her trump card. She took a deep breath of dusty, stale air as she rose from her seat. For a moment, she feared she would faint.

Come now, Emily. Be firm.

"Well, I am sorry to have bothered you, Mr. Harris. I was really only getting a second estimate. I already have a proposal from another architect — a Mr. McAllister. Perhaps you know him?"

"Mr. McAllister?" The weedy man's eyes narrowed. "Duncan McAllister?"

"Yes, I believe that is his Christian name. He gave me a very good price."

"I will wager that he did. Please, Mrs. Lewis, sit down. There is something I believe you should know."

Obediently, Emily sat again. She braced herself for the words she knew were coming next.

"Mr. McAllister has something of a poor reputation among his fellow architects," Mr. Harris began in his thin voice. "It is shocking, really, how one man's behavior can stain the integrity of an entire profession."

"Shocking, yes."

"Do you know the Earl and Countess of Langdon?"

Emily forced herself to smile. "I am afraid not, Mr. Harris. Despite living in Mayfair, I do not move in their circles."

"Then perhaps you have not heard the story of their conservatory, which Mr. McAllister designed. Three months ago, it tumbled to the ground! The width of the supporting beams had not been calculated properly. It is just fortunate that no one was inside it at the time."

"Yes, indeed," said Emily, wondering acerbically how Clare could have forgotten to mention such a spectacular accident in her letters. "How dreadful! I cannot believe it!"

"You would be wise to do so," he murmured. "In fact, I know other unfortunate stories regarding Mr. McAllister's work. A Mr. Tarnwell told me personally about the kitchen he had hired Mr. McAllister to build in Warwickshire — it was prone to chimney fires. And there was a façade in Somerset where a pillar cracked because it was too heavy for the soft soil on which it stood."

He described the ridiculous fabrications

in rapid detail, pausing neither to think nor to breathe — rather like a child reciting a poem.

It was very like the manner in which Simon had tried to cover up his indiscretions. One thing her marriage had taught her was how to recognize a liar.

Emily nodded, schooling her features into a suitable expression of dismay. It was clear that Mr. Harris himself was the source of the rumors.

"I am just glad you came to see me before signing a contract of any sort with McAllister." Mr. Harris's voice oozed false sympathy. "He likely quoted you a price within your budget, did he not?"

Emily nodded. How she longed to slap the smirk from Mr. Harris's face!

"He will do anything to meet a client's budget — even provide hurried designs and hire incompetent workers," Harris added.

Emily tried to sound grateful. "Thank you so much, Mr. Harris, for warning me. But what is the benefit to you of spreading such lurid tales of your profession?"

Harris breathed a theatrical sigh. "It is a risk, I know, but I believe the good of my clients outweighs the drawbacks."

"It does not do your business any harm, either, I suppose, to denigrate the work of a competitor?" Emily kept her voice sweet, despite her fury.

Nonetheless, the architect scowled. "Are you insinuating something, Mrs. Lewis?"

Emily sensed she was about to overstep the mark, and stood. "Not at all, Mr. Harris," she said. "Please do not take offense. I am beholden to you for sharing this information."

"And if you do decide to go through with those renovations, and are willing to extend your budget, please keep me in mind." He stood and held out his hand. Emily pretended she did not see it.

"I shall, Mr. Harris," she said, smoothing her skirt in an effort to still her own hand's trembling. "I will remember you, without a doubt."

Emily left the house as quickly as she could. Her stomach was still quaking with disgust at Nigel Harris's tactics as the coachman handed her up into the hired cabriolet. But she exulted as she collapsed against the worn velvet squabs. She had found the source of Mr. McAllister's troubles!

Her excitement almost dowsed her fear of dining with the architect the following night.

Ten

This evening looked likely to become the longest one of Emily's life. Although she and Mr. McAllister had had little time to speak since she and Alex had arrived, she found she had not been able to take her eyes from him in the interim.

He wore a double-breasted dress coat of brown wool whose trim fit clearly revealed the strong shoulders of a boxer. It had surprised Emily to learn that a man as gentle as Mr. McAllister should have a taste for pugilism — a taste that also, no doubt, accounted for the fine figure he cut in his buff pantaloons.

Such thoughts led inexorably to others. No matter how hard she tried to suppress them, memories of that afternoon in the studio would intrude. The intense comfort she had felt in his arms. The heat that had suffused her as he kissed her. And his stricken face when she had withdrawn from his embrace.

At least tonight she would be able to make up, in some small way, for the coolness she had been forced to show. But first, she had to find an opportunity to speak to him in private. The unpleasant news about Mr. Harris would not be the sort of thing he would want to share with the entire company, she suspected.

At the moment, Mr. McAllister was chatting with his parents, seated on the sofa. The elder Mr. McAllister was solidly built, with the wide hazel eyes his children had inherited, a ruddy complexion, and abundant silvery hair. His expertly tied neckcloth and coat of blue superfine, while not perhaps in the latest mode, were still fashionable, and his boots gleamed. He smiled seldom and observed everything with a careful merchant's eye. Emily found him forbidding — he reminded her a great deal of her own father.

Mrs. McAllister, on the other hand, charmed all and sundry. As warm as her husband was cool, she had a quiet, quick wit — a muted version of her son's sense of the absurd. She also seemed the likely source of her children's distinctive hair; although hers was now mainly silver, streaks of ginger remained.

Penny, seated in a small chair next to her parents, was elegant as always in a gown of green silk, but she was nibbling her lower lip. Several times, she looked pleadingly at

Alex, who had spent most of the evening drifting about the sitting room like a windblown leaf.

Although dinner was the only thing that anyone would admit to anticipating — the enticing aroma of roast beef was already rising from the kitchen — the air almost vibrated with greater tensions. Emily's heart went out to her brother and Penny. She remembered the day when Simon had offered for her; she had been as taut as a violin string. Unlike Penny, however, she had been hoping her father would refuse.

"I cannae ken how you managed to capture wee Susannah so well." Mrs. McAllister's soft voice startled Emily, as she had not seen the older woman approach. The McAllister men appeared deep in discussion of some political matter, and Mrs. McAllister had slipped over to Emily's side. "I feel as though she were about to leap off the canvas and join us."

"Thank you, Mrs. McAllister," Emily said, with only a faint flush of embarrassment.

"Have you been a professional painter long?"

"I am not precisely a professional," Emily said with what she hoped was a dismissive laugh. "I paint for my own amusement, but your son happened to see a few of my works and asked me to paint this portrait in exchange for some work he was doing on my house."

"So 'twas a barter arrangement?" Mrs. McAllister's brows drew together in a slight frown.

"Yes, I suppose that is the correct term."

Mrs. McAllister turned her back to the others and leaned toward Emily. "I know 'tis bold, Lady Tuncliffe, but tell me: do you know whether my son is taking on many such jobs?"

Emily blinked. "I do not know for a fact, Mrs. McAllister, but I would think it rather unlikely."

"It is just that he looks so drawn. I am concerned that his foray into architecture has not been a success. His father so wanted him to become a partner in the firm, and I took Duncan's side against Ian. We had terrible rows over it, but in the end, Duncan and I prevailed. I so wanted him to be happy in his profession."

"He is happy," Emily chimed in, eager to diminish the kind woman's fears. "When he was supervising the work on my house, he behaved as though there was nowhere else on earth he would rather be." She thought of her encounter with Mr. Harris.

"And I believe his business may just be about to take a turn for the better."

Mrs. McAllister smiled. "It pleases me to hear it. For a short period after he lost dear Olivia, I was afraid he would never recover his optimistic disposition."

"Her death must have been a dreadful shock."

"Duncan bore it well — he has always been a strong person. And, of course, he had Penny for company. They were always the best of friends, even as children."

"What about your other son? Are he and Mr. McAllister close?"

"Neil and Duncan? As unalike as chalk and cheese, those two are!" Mrs. McAllister chortled. "And yet, they seem to rub along quite well. Neil, thank goodness, has prospered in the business even though, at one time, he wanted to become a clergyman. He is a quiet sort, not given to the capers that Duncan is."

Emily smiled.

"When Duncan was younger, oh, the grand buildings he used to sketch on scraps of paper!" Mrs. McAllister recalled. "Cathedrals and libraries, enormous estates and fanciful pavilions of glass. He used to speak of designing an entire village so that every person — even the lowest-paid factory worker or farmhand — would have a small house with a garden and a solid roof."

Emily was charmed. She could well imagine Mr. McAllister creating castles in the air.

From the corner of her eye, she noticed Alex and the elder Mr. McAllister leaving the room and heading for the study. A moment later, Penny called her mother over to her side.

Emily, left alone, sipped her tea and closed her eyes. After so many years of spending days at a time alone, she still found parties — even small ones — slightly overwhelming.

"Lady Tuncliffe?" The younger Mr. McAllister's voice interrupted her thoughts. "Are you all right?"

"Yes, thank you," she said, looking up at him. She clenched her hands together in her lap, willing her nervousness away. "I am just resting my eyes, as my grandmother used to say."

"I see that Lord Rossley has sequestered himself with my father. Never a pleasant task at the best of times, and it would be particularly daunting in circumstances such as these." He sat down in the chair next to her and leaned back.

He seemed determined to be cordial. Perhaps he bore her less ill will than she had feared.

"So Penny has told you what is afoot?"

Mr. McAllister grinned. "Told me? She practically shouted the news at me. She is overjoyed by the idea, and I share her enthusiasm. I would be pleased to welcome Rossley to the family."

"I feel just the same toward Penny."

Glancing toward the other side of the room, she saw Penny and Mrs. McAllister deep in conversation. There would be no better time for Emily to share what she had learned about Mr. Harris.

"I have some news regarding your business," she whispered. "I think you will be glad to hear it — well, angry at first, but ultimately glad."

He leaned forward and rested his forearms on his knees, his face alarmingly close to hers. "About my business? I am all ears."

Emily took a deep breath. "I have discovered that another architect has been spreading lies about you and your work. He seems to be doing it to increase the profits of his own practice."

Mr. McAllister frowned. "Who is this architect?"

"A man named Nigel Harris."

"Harris!" He grimaced. "I should have suspected someone like him at the root of this. The man has the ethics of a wild dog. But how did you learn of this?"

Emily told him of her conversation with Lady Farnham.

"But Harris was only one of the sources Lady Farnham mentioned," Mr. McAllister remarked. "I cannot jump to the conclusion that it is he, tempting as it is to do so."

Emily grinned. "Yes, you can! I have all the proof you need, short of a signed affidavit."

"What do you mean?"

"I visited his office, and he practically hanged himself in my presence. He repeated every lie Lady Farnham had relayed, and some others as well."

"You went to Harris's office?" Far from delighted, Mr. McAllister looked ready to explode.

"Yes." What could be the source of his rancor?

"That was a preposterously risky thing to do!"

Emily shot a glance at Penny and Mrs. McAllister, but they did not appear to have noticed his outburst.

"It was not risky at all." Suddenly, she

realized the source of his apprehension. "You see, I used a false name! There is no chance at all that he can connect me to the Langdons, or Simon, or you."

"Thank God for that, at least. But it was still foolhardy."

"Why?"

He sighed. "Harris is an unsavory character. I knew him at Harrow — the wellspring of all evil, I am beginning to believe — and later at Oxford. In fact, our past acquaintance may be the source of his current animosity toward me."

"I must admit, I wondered why he should have singled you out among all the architects in London. I cannot imagine you doing anyone harm. What transpired between the two of you?"

Mr. McAllister's voice was grim. "The whole story is not fit supper party conversation."

"Then tell me the expurgated version."

His large hands were clenched on his knees, the knuckles white. "I came upon Harris behind an Oxford pub, trying to take advantage of a barmaid. She was obviously not encouraging his intentions. I intervened, and he did not appreciate it."

"What did he do?" Emily tried to picture the scene.

"Well, he tried to give me a black eye. Fortunately, even then I had about four inches and two stone on him." Mr. McAllister frowned. "But this is all ancient history. I can't believe that Harris has carried a grudge against me all these years."

"Simon was the same. He never remembered a kindness and never forgot an injury."

"Thank you for sharing this information with me, Lady Tuncliffe — even if you did take a foolish risk to confirm it." He shook his head. "If I had known, I would have forbidden you to do anything so outlandish."

"I do not recognize your authority to forbid me to do anything." Emily's voice was crisp.

Mr. McAllister sighed and ran a hand through his tousled hair. "You are right, of course. I made a poor choice of words, and I already know that it is almost impossible to dissuade you from any course of action that you have embarked upon. Forgive me."

Emily nodded. "Let us not argue over each other's words and actions, Mr. McAllister. What is done is done. The important thing is that you now know the source of the rumors."

He laughed. "How sensible you are, Lady Tuncliffe. This is indeed marvelous news, and I have not thanked you properly. You do not know what a yoke you have removed from my shoulders. Now that I know the source of my troubles, it should be a simple matter to stanch the rumors."

"What will you do?"

"Confront Harris at the earliest opportunity, and convince him of the wisdom of publishing a notice in the newspapers correcting the falsehoods he has spread."

Emily nodded. "So the matter appears closed."

"It does. And once it is closed entirely, I will be able, I hope, to turn my attention to other things." A grin split his ruddy features, sending a thrilling crackle down Emily's skin.

Would this feeling always be there between them?

After a moment, Mr. McAllister glanced toward the doorway through which his father and Alex had disappeared. "They do seem to be spending a long time in discussion," he remarked in an odd voice. "Penny must be distraught."

Emily was both relieved and sorry that he had shifted his attention. "Such evenings are always fraught with high emotion. I am glad that I could be here to support Alex."

"I am pleased you came." He paused. "After our discussion in your studio the other day, I was afraid that my ungentlemanly actions —"

Emily held up her hand. "Please, Mr. McAllister, do not apologize. It is I who should be sorry for burdening you with my past woes."

"Do not think twice about it. I am only glad I could be of service." He paused. "I hope you will continue to consider me a friend and, when need be, a confidant."

Emily smiled as happiness suffused her. "I would be honored. And I hope that you will do the same."

"I shall."

A small silence fell between them.

"I hope you do not mind that we did not also invite your parents," Mr. McAllister said. "I mentioned the idea to Rossley, but he was not in favor of it."

"I suppose he told you that it would be unwise to have them both in the same room, if you valued your fine china?"

He laughed. "Something to that effect. Is the animosity between your parents truly so intense?"

"Yes, sadly. At Clarissa and Matthew's

wedding, we had to seat them at opposite ends of the church so they would not hiss and spit at each other. Honestly, I love Mama dearly and I respect Papa, but the two of them are worse than a pair of territorial cats."

Emily thought of her parents' failed marriage, as she always did, with regret. It had foundered largely on her mother's complaints that the marquess was too set in his ways — and too fond of giving orders.

Perhaps most partnerships between men and women were doomed to fall into a similar pattern. Simon had considered her little better than property. And even Mr. McAllister, kind though he was, seemed prone to making pronouncements.

Granted, Clarissa and Matthew seemed to have a more equal partnership. But then, there was the exception to every rule, and Clarissa was notoriously strong-willed.

Before Emily could pursue this line of thought further, the elder Mr. McAllister and Alex returned to the sitting room. Alex's ear-to-ear grin told her everything she needed to know, and she had to clench her hands on the arms of her chair to keep from leaping up to congratulate him.

"May I have your attention?" Penny's father said in stentorian tones that Emily could well imagine silencing the clerks in his Edinburgh emporium.

The chatter ceased.

"I have just had a most interesting conversation with young Rossley here," he announced. "It appears that he fervently wishes to marry our wee lass."

Penny giggled at this description. "I am nae wee nor a lass," she protested.

"You'll always be my wee lass, and you would be wise not to forget it," her father replied. For the first time, Emily sensed that his severity was more for show than anything.

"Now, as I was saying before my ill-mannered offspring interrupted me, Lord Rossley has made a heartfelt offer for Penelope's hand. While I am saddened to see yet another of my children tempted away to a life among the English" — he looked at his son — "it would take a much sterner man than I to deny a union that both partners so obviously desire. And as Penny will in the future become a marchioness, there was nae reasonable objection I could raise. So it is with great pleasure that I announce —"

"Ach, Ian, just say it!" Mrs. McAllister cried, embracing her daughter. "I am so happy for you, Penny!"

"As am I," Emily said, rising from her chair and crossing the room. "Welcome to the Denham family, my dear. We are a strange brood, but I hope you will like us."

"I already do," Penny said, as a happy tear skidded down her cheek. "Thank you," she whispered, just before Alex enveloped her in a tight hug.

"Congratulations, Rossley," Duncan McAllister said, extending his hand to shake his soon-to-be brother-in-law's when Alex finally relinquished his grip on a rather breathless Penny. "Welcome to Clan McAllister."

In the midst of the ensuing hubbub of congratulations and exclamations, Libby announced that supper was served. As befitted a formal occasion, the gentlemen would escort the ladies to the dining room. As Mrs. McAllister joined her husband, Alex proudly took Penny's arm in his.

That left the younger Mr. McAllister to accompany Emily.

"May I?" he asked, extending his elbow. In his glance, she saw the embers of the warmth with which he had gazed at her in the studio.

He had not given up. And, knowing him, it was unlikely that he would quit his pursuit just because she had asked him to.

What could she do?

"Lady Tuncliffe?" he prompted. The company was waiting for her and Mr. McAllister to lead them into the dining room, as Emily was the highest ranking person in attendance. There was nothing for it but to do as propriety demanded.

"By all means, I would be honored," she replied, taking Mr. McAllister's arm. He held her close to his side as they left the room.

Her arm tingled through her white satin glove where it pressed against Mr. McAllister's wool coat. It felt utterly natural to walk this way.

"What a joyous day this is, Mr. McAllister," she remarked as they entered the dining room. She had to talk, to prevent herself from thinking.

"As we are soon to be related," he said as he pulled out her chair, "may I suggest that you call me Duncan?"

Emily swallowed. Calling him by his first name would denote much greater intimacy than was wise. It was dangerous to start along a path she could not follow to the end.

And yet, it was so tempting.

"Thank you, Duncan," she said, savoring his name like a mouthful of fine wine.

"And you must call me Emily."

"I hope I will have the opportunity to do so often in the future," he said, that compelling light still gleaming in the depths of his hazel eyes.

"Of course you will. We will be friends and relations, after all." She tried to keep her voice firm but light.

"Of course. Friends and relations." His voice was gently mocking, but he said no more.

Emily's stomach was in turmoil as she sat down to the table. What had she just allowed to happen?

The mantua maker clucked her tongue. "It will be a challenge to find something flattering with that flaming hair, *n'est-ce pas?*" she exclaimed in the most ridiculous imitation of a French accent imaginable. Emily would wager her mother's pearls that Madame Tissot hailed from somewhere much nearer Leeds than Lyons.

"Pay her no heed," Emily whispered in Penny's ear as the portly dressmaker toddled to the back of the shop to find some sketches. "Your hair is charming, and if she cannot find a suitable fabric to set it off, we will take our custom elsewhere!"

Mrs. McAllister, who had overheard this

exchange, nodded in agreement. "I am glad you are with us, Lady Tuncliffe. With your artistic eye, we are certain to find just the right wedding dress!"

"I will do my best, Mrs. McAllister. Although, truth to tell, I am not much of a shopper."

"Emily, this gown would look fetching on you!" cried Penny, pointing toward a dress of bishop's blue embossed silk displayed on a mannequin. The gown had an overskirt of feathery gold lace, and similar lacework bordered the deep, square neckline.

"We are here to find a dress for you, not for me," Emily said, wagging her finger. Although she did not need a new dress, she went over to the mannequin to examine the garment.

"Penny is right, Lady Tuncliffe — 'twould bring out your eyes. And such a dramatic color with your golden hair! You would look just like a china doll."

Emily fingered the soft, rich fabric. It was lovely. However, she still needed to be cautious with her funds. She was by no means destitute, but neither did the small widow's portion from Simon's estate give her the means to live like a princess.

"It is pretty," she said. "But I am afraid

that my household budget does not extend to any new wardrobe items at the moment. The renovations were my major expenditure for this year."

"Duncan would enjoy seeing you wear such a gown." Penny's voice was teasing.

"Mr. McAllister? Why would he care what I wear?" Panic raced through Emily's veins. What had Duncan told his sister?

Beads of sweat broke out on her brow.

"Emily! Certainly you have noticed the way he looks at you." Penny smiled, her face guileless.

Emily sighed with relief. Penny had simply made a few observations.

The faux Frenchwoman emerged from the back of the shop, her arms full of color plates. "I believe *mamzelle* might find this style attractive, made up in a rich green, *comme ça.*" The dressmaker placed an illustration and a swath of emerald satin on the table in front of Penny.

"Green does become me," Penny murmured, picking up the fabric and laying it against her hand. "What do you think, Emily? You have such skill with colors."

To Emily's immense relief, the patterns and fabrics distracted the McAllister women's attention from any discussion of a relationship between her and Duncan. Du-

189

tifully, she examined each plate and fabric scrap in turn, giving her considered opinion on them.

"Mr. Harris is working. Is he expecting you?" Harris's housekeeper was reserved, and had barely opened the front door beyond a crack.

Duncan stood his ground. "No. I realize this is a bit presumptuous, but Mr. Harris and I were acquaintances at school. I would like to meet with him this afternoon, if possible."

The grim-faced woman glanced at Duncan's card. "It is unusual that you do not have an appointment, Mr. McAllister."

Duncan ground his teeth in annoyance. It would not be surprising if Harris was desperate for clients, if this was the way his staff treated unknown callers. Libby would have had a guest inside enjoying a cup of tea long before now.

"Would it be possible for you to ask Mr. Harris whether he would be inclined to meet a caller?"

"Yes, I suppose." She made to close the door.

"May I wait in the foyer?" Duncan would be demmed if he would stand on Harris's front step.

The taciturn housekeeper opened the door with a begrudging sigh. "Suit yourself, sir."

Duncan stood in the dim, dank foyer as the housekeeper wandered off in search of Harris. The chamber was papered in an unappealing shade of puce, and the flagstones were chipped and dull. If he had the commission to renovate it, he would replace the dark stone with pink-veined marble, and use a much lighter color on the walls to make the space appear larger.

The muted tones of a discussion at the back of the house grew louder as he bided his time in the foyer. By the time the housekeeper reappeared, Duncan had remodeled half the building in his mind.

"I am sorry, sir, but Mr. Harris is unavailable."

At this reply, Duncan lost his temper.

"I believe I will make him available," he muttered as he stalked past the housekeeper and down the corridor whence she had come.

"Sir! Please, sir!" He ignored the servant's agitated cries as he headed for a doorway at the far end of the house, from which a pool of faint light emanated.

Pushing the door fully open, he saw Harris seated at a scarred, largely empty desk. The hearth behind him was dusty with cold embers; the room felt disused.

"McAllister." The man's face betrayed no emotion. "Please sit down."

"I prefer to stand."

Harris shrugged. "As you wish. I must say, it is a surprise to see you. Looking for some advice from a more seasoned architect? I am always happy to share my expertise, although I do wish you had made an appointment."

Duncan's mood had been dark before he entered the room. Now it was pitch black. Not only had Harris the gall to impugn his reputation behind his back, but he also had the temerity to insult Duncan to his face.

"Forgive my lack of social graces." Duncan did not bother to hide his sarcasm.

Harris had not aged well. His skin hung sallow on his bony frame and his nose, bulbous and red, provided the only color in his face.

A drinker, most likely.

"Business not going well?" the other architect asked. "I hear that you have lost a few choice commissions in the last few months."

"Oh, you have? Where did you hear that?"

Harris lowered his gaze to a sheaf of papers on his desk. "Here and there. People talk."

"So they do. For instance, I have heard that you have been saying some fascinating things."

Dull blotches rose on the man's pale cheeks. "Such as?"

"Such as the fact that the conservatory I designed for the Earl of Langdon came crashing down of its own accord. I was most interested to hear that."

"You mean it did not? Well, then, I am in error."

"Whatever gave you the impression that it had?"

"I heard things."

"Did you also hear that a small villa I designed near Brighton immediately developed a cracked foundation?" Duncan chose a story he had discovered in a conversation with Lady Farnham, but which Harris had not told Emily. Above all, he wanted to avoid giving Harris any reason to suspect that Emily was the source of his information.

Harris sighed and looked up. "Stop playing the innocent. You obviously know that I have been spreading stories, so let us get to the point."

"I would love to do that. What point, exactly, were you trying to make? Is this revenge for the serving girl at Oxford?"

The other man wrinkled his forehead. "The serving girl? Oh yes, I was demmed foxed at the time. I had completely forgotten you charging on me like some Arthurian knight."

Harris's voice was far too casual, Duncan thought. Nigel hadn't forgotten a thing.

"Do not flatter yourself," Harris continued. "This plan had nothing to do with you."

"Nothing to do with me!" Duncan reached across the desk and grabbed his old enemy by his faded lapels. "You almost made me a bankrupt. I would say that has everything to do with me. I could have you hauled into the courts for slander."

"Such cases are demmed hard to prove." The other man's voice shook slightly, but otherwise he stood his ground. "If hearsay was that powerful, I could have you in front of a magistrate on charges of assault." He nodded towards Duncan's fists, which still clenched his coat.

Duncan relaxed his hold. "If I am to be brought to court for assault, I should make it worth my while and do more than just wrinkle your jacket."

"Is that a threat?" Harris's voice was less bold now. He had always been the worst kind of bully: all talk and no action.

"No." Duncan released his grip and sat down on a hard wooden chair. "Much as I would enjoy fighting you, it would solve nothing. What I would rather do is find out your motive. Why did you do it?"

"To solve my own business woes!" Harris exploded, coming out from behind the desk and waving his arms. "Look around you! Does this look like the premises of a wildly successful architect?"

Duncan had to admit that it did not.

"I cannot even keep staff worthy of a reference, as I can afford to pay them so little."

"So you are having trouble getting work, and you decided to steal my commissions by denigrating me in front of potential clients. But why me?"

"Why not you? I had never particularly liked you, and you seemed to be doing well. I assumed you would never notice a commission or two gone wrong."

"A commission or two? More like twenty or thirty!" Duncan was appalled at the man's arrogant disregard for the rules of fair play.

"I had to increase my efforts."

"Why?" A thought struck him. "I know that Mrs. Tepper's commission for a new façade was awarded to Sir David Price, not to you. And the commission for the new vestibule for St. Stephen's Church went to Martin Fisher. You have been doing a fine job of destroying my reputation, but it has not been paying off in work, has it?"

"No!" Harris's fist slammed down on his desk. "Ridiculous fools! I have spent hours, days, weeks — *months* — meeting with these foolish women and their pinch-penny husbands, wandering through rotting church basements with demented vicars, calculating estimates. But when I present my drawings, the wretched clients sniff and say they are unsuitable!" Nigel's voice was strained, almost hysterical.

"What displeases them?"

"If I knew that, I would not be in this fix, would I?" Harris rolled his eyes to the ceiling. "If it hadn't been for my demmed uncle, it would not matter so much."

"What do you mean?"

"He wanted me to follow in his footsteps. Sold me his business. After teaching me the rudiments, he passed on, leaving me with a handful of doddering clients and a mountain of unpaid bills."

"And you have been trying to pay the creditors?"

"When I can." Harris scowled. "They howl incessantly for money. One even had the temerity to approach me in Boodle's and harangue me while I was in the middle of a game. Said I should not be wasting his money."

Duncan sympathized with the unknown creditor. Harris, it appeared, was as lazy and shiftless as he had been in school. It was apparent that he had made no effort to improve his skills, preferring to blame his lack of success on ill-tempered clients and his lack of money on unreasonable creditors.

"Your debt is not my problem. Your lies are."

"I will stop spreading them immediately."

"That will be insufficient."

Harris raised watery eyes to his. "What else do you want, McAllister?"

"Satisfaction." Duncan paused. "I want you to publish a notice in the major papers, apologizing for any unfounded stories you may have spread regarding my reputation."

What little color existed in Harris's face disappeared. "And how will that make me look?"

"Like the lying scoundrel you are."

Harris scowled. "And if I refuse?"

"I will publish my own notice. But I promise you that it will be even less helpful to your reputation than your own is likely to be."

"I could sue you for libel."

"Not if I am careful."

Harris walked back around his desk and slumped into the chair. "Fine. I will do it. But I urge you to think twice about this demand. It could ruin me."

"Do not put the blame at my door. You have ruined yourself." Duncan stood. He was anxious to escape this house, where he felt increasingly uncomfortable. Something undefinable about Harris — something more than his unpleasant personality — set Duncan's teeth on edge. "If you will excuse me, I have an appointment to make some calls with my sister. I will see myself out."

Penny looked up into the curricle and laughed. "Honestly, Duncan, it is only a mantua maker's shop, not Dante's Inferno."

Duncan shook his head again. "My opinion will be of little use to you. I should stay with the carriage."

"Young Bob is more than able to watch the rig, are you not?" Penny addressed the tiger perched on the back seat.

"Yes, miss. I can do it!"

"There, you see?" Penny's voice was cajoling. "Really, all I need is your opinion on the last dress Mother wants me to choose for my trousseau. I have narrowed the decision down to two styles. We will be out of the shop and back on the street before you have time to panic."

"But —"

"Honestly, Duncan, have you lost every ounce of your good humor? I swear, I hardly know you any more!"

He frowned. Penny had a point. He suspected he had been something of a trial over the last week, since he first learned of Harris's slander.

He held up his hands in mock surrender.

"If you decide to cry off this marriage, you could always become a highwayman," Duncan said, looking behind him for oncoming horses before jumping down from his seat. "You have pried me from my post when no gun could do the trick."

"This will not take long, I promise."

Soon they were settled in comfortable chairs in the cluttered but cozy shop. If only the mantua maker had not insisted on calling him *"meez-sure,"* it would have been quite a painless excursion.

"Are these the designs you liked, *mamzelle?*" Madame Tissot asked, handing two fashion plates to Penny.

"Yes, this is one," Penny said, waving a drawing of a gold-colored evening gown. "What do you think, Duncan?" she asked, passing the plate to him.

He considered the drawing for what he estimated was a reasonable length of time. "Very nice, Penny. I like it."

Penny rolled her eyes. "Are you just trying to placate me?"

"Perhaps. Would you rather I returned to the carriage?"

She gave him a playful swat with her fan. "I would rather you gave me a worthwhile opinion."

"Truly, Penny, I think it would suit you. The color would work well with your hair. But why decide? Father and Mother are determined to send you off in style, and I am certain they would urge you to buy both."

Penny laughed. "That is true. If Mother were here instead of having tea with Alex's mother, she would likely do just that. I suppose I am just unused to having a limitless clothing budget!"

Looking at the other drawing in her lap, she signaled the mantua maker. "This is not the gown I had in mind. The one that intrigued me was a sprigged muslin day dress with rosettes on the sleeves."

"Rosettes? Ah yes, I know zee very one. Just a minute."

As the little round seamstress bounded to the back of the shop and began sifting through a pile of sketches on a long table, Penny nudged Duncan.

"Remember the gown Emily so admired? It is still here!"

"The one she said her budget would not permit her to buy?"

"Yes — right over there on that mannequin. Do you not think she was foolish to pass it up?"

Duncan turned in his chair and followed Penny's line of sight. And for the first time in his life, his own imagination knocked him speechless.

The gown was an arresting shade of purplish blue, with an outer layer of fine gold lace. Tiny cap sleeves fell away to a sweeping neckline.

On the mannequin, the dress was nice enough. But clinging to Emily's soft curves — the curves he remembered beneath his hands from their embrace . . .

He coughed in an effort to clear the sudden tightness in his chest.

"What do you think?"

"About what?" Duncan struggled to keep any evidence of his wayward thoughts from his expression, but Penny nonetheless gave him a queer look.

"About the gown! Dinnae you agree it would look fetching on Emily?"

He nodded to his sister, but addressed his next remark to the shop owner. "That gown on the mannequin — what is its price?"

Madame Tissot turned from her search for the missing plate. "Zee blue one? It is eighteen pounds, *meez-sure.*"

Eighteen pounds. A year ago — six months ago — Duncan would have paid that price without a moment's thought. But given the state of his funds at the moment, he could not do it. Unlike his sister, he was not trolling the shops with his parents' blunt in his purse — nor would he want to be.

And even if Harris's notice in the papers succeeded, it would be months before Duncan had much cash on hand.

But that dress was made for Emily. And he owed her a proper thank you for her help in trapping Harris.

Suddenly, he remembered Piers Sherrington's offer to purchase the Delft vase. He had resisted it because the vase had been a gift from a satisfied client. He kept it above his desk to buoy his confidence on the days when he feared he would never win another commission. It had cheered him immensely over the last few months.

But he had just discovered something else that would lift his spirits ten times better.

"Would you be willing to extend me credit for the dress, just for a few days?" he asked the seamstress, digging into his pocket and extracting several coins and a crumpled bank note. "I could leave — let's see — one pound, three shillings, and sixpence as security."

At the mention of money, the proprietress scurried over. "No security is necessary, sir," she said, her French accent momentarily forgotten. "I would be happy to extend you credit. Would you like to try the gown on, miss?"

Penny, who had been observing this exchange with increasing amusement, chuckled. "I would be pleased to, but I do not believe the gown is for me."

"Not for you?" The seamstress frowned,

then slowly looked Duncan up and down.

Penny's laughter rang off the walls. "I do not think the color would complement my brother's hair either!"

Duncan's mouth twitched. "But I do think the sleeves would show off my slender arms. Just the thing to wear to a fine night of entertainment at Gentleman Jackson's!"

With that, the siblings collapsed in mirth, much to Madame Tissot's evident bewilderment.

When she could finally catch her breath, Penny explained. "I believe my brother wants to buy this dress for a friend. I shan't mention her name, because I suspect the gift is to be a surprise."

Duncan nodded. "And, knowing the lady, I am not certain she would want it to be common knowledge that I am in the habit of purchasing gowns for her."

The proprietress raised her shoulders in a fair approximation of a Gallic shrug. "It does not matter to me. But what does the lady look like? Alterations might be necessary."

Penny stood up and motioned her brother to do likewise. Standing next to him, she put her hand on the top of her head, leveled it against his shoulder, and stepped away. She studied the position of her hand.

"I believe she does not quite reach your shoulder, which I do," she said to Duncan. "So she is perhaps two inches shorter than I?"

Duncan moved his hand about that distance below Penny's, then shifted it across his body to his chest. He considered. Yes, that was roughly where her head had rested when he had embraced her.

This endeavor was beginning to seem indelicate.

"Yes, that appears right," he said, his voice gruff even to his own ears.

"And does she have the same build as your sister?"

Duncan considered. Both Penny and Emily were slim, but Emily was . . . different, somehow.

Deuced awkward process, this. He was certain his ears were turning pink. What a thing to have to discuss in front of one's *sister!*

Penny, as usual, saved him. "Yes, although she is somewhat more . . . curvaceous than I am." She paused, then gave her brother a sly glance. "Would you not say so, Duncan?"

"Yes, yes, I think you are quite correct,

Penny." He turned on his heel. He would buy the dress, but he would be demmed if he would sit around while the women discussed the details. "I am finding it somewhat stuffy in here. Would you mind providing Madame Tissot with the rest of the information she requires to alter the gown?"

He swore he could feel Penny's grin through the blue superfine of his coat. "I would not mind at all. Will you be in the carriage?"

"Yes!" he bellowed, and fled. Penny's delighted laughter hounded him all the way to the curb.

"What am I to do, Clare?" Emily felt like howling.

"Try it on, I would say." Clarissa was ensconced on a slipper chair in Emily's bedroom, beneath the painting of the washerwoman. Emily had succeeded in getting her way on that score, at least; Duncan had not convinced her to hang any of her paintings in the public rooms of her town house.

But how could she resist this generous gift? She fingered the luxurious silk of the gown she had coveted in Madame Tissot's shop.

"If that is the best advice you can give, you should have stayed in Oxfordshire," Emily said.

"What, and miss Alex's betrothal party? I should say not! It is bad enough that in the short time I have been away, he has gone from callow schoolboy to love-struck swain, and I missed the transformation. I would not have missed tonight's entertainment for the world, even if I will be confined to the company of the sober matrons on the fringes of the dance floor. Even if it were proper for me to dance in my condition, I doubt I should last long."

"Are you still ill in the mornings?"

"Yes, but it is not as dreadful lately." Clarissa frowned at her sister. "Don't try to divert the conversation, Em. You should at least try the dress on. It is rude to refuse a gift."

"But this is no mere gift! This dress must have cost at least fifteen pounds. I did not even have the nerve to ask Madame Tissot its price."

"Mr. McAllister would not have purchased it for you if he could not afford it. Did you not say that his business was poised to recover?"

"Yes, thank heavens." Nigel Harris's notice had appeared in all the major papers a

207

week ago. And, according to Penny, clients had already begun coming round to the small Chelsea house.

Emily had had no direct contact with Duncan since the night Penny's father had accepted Alex's suit. When Duncan had taken her arm to lead her into dinner, and asked her to call him by his Christian name, a stab of longing had shaken her. Getting too close to Duncan McAllister would be bad for her peace of mind.

As a result, she had politely declined a subsequent invitation to supper. And she had agreed to accompany Penny and Alex to the theater the previous evening only when she had ascertained that Duncan would be elsewhere.

"You played a role in helping Mr. McAllister find Mr. Harris — a rather large role, it sounds like." Clarissa smiled. "It was very brave of you, Em. A few months ago, you would not have had the confidence."

"I am learning." Emily smiled.

"It is only natural that he would want to thank you for your help."

Emily gazed at the dress, spread across the embroidered cream counterpane of her bed. She had treated herself to few pretty things since emerging from mourning several months ago. And nothing in her wardrobe compared to this.

Once again, she picked up the card that the messenger had delivered along with the gown. *In gratitude and friendship. DM.*

Clarissa was right. It was a perfectly reasonable gift and an innocuous letter.

Gratitude and friendship. Not one whiff of the intimacy they had shared in her studio. That was a good thing, was it not?

"Em? What's wrong?"

"Nothing. I was just thinking that you are correct. It was very kind of Duncan to send this dress, and I should do him the courtesy of at least trying it on."

As the words escaped her lips, she wished she could take them back. But it was too late — Clare, who missed little, pounced.

"Duncan?"

Mortified, Emily nodded. She sat down on the bed.

"It appears that Alex is not the only Denham whose romantic affairs have bloomed while I have been rusticating in Oxfordshire." Clarissa waggled her eyebrows.

Emily smiled at her sister's antics, and kept her voice light. "There is nothing romantic about it. Mr. McAllister and I are to be related, after all. He invited me to call him Duncan on the night his father accepted Alex's suit. I daresay he will ask you to do the same."

Clare's laughter bubbled through the room. "Perhaps, but I doubt I will blush quite so prettily when I address him."

"Clare, don't laugh! It is no laughing matter."

Instantly, her sister sobered. "Is your interest not reciprocated, then?"

"I have no interest!" Emily stopped. She could not lie, especially to her sister. "Well, that is not precisely true. I do find Duncan . . . Mr. McAllister . . . most appealing. He is charming and, and . . ."

"— and a *beau ideal?*" Clarissa's mirth threatened to burst forth once more.

"What business have you noticing such things? You are a married woman!"

"I am married, but I'm not blind."

"But I am a recent widow, and I should be blind."

Clare crossed the room and sat down beside her sister. "Is that the problem, Em? Simon has been gone two years. No one would speak ill of you."

"That is not all." Emily's voice was quiet. "I am also afraid."

"Of what?"

"I have worked so hard to shape a new life for myself — refurbishing this house, even painting to earn an income. I am loath to give up my independence."

"You need give nothing up, right away. Take the time to get to know each other — quietly, if you are concerned about the propriety of appearing in public. Something may develop."

Emily could not bear her sister's well-intentioned advice any longer without speaking. "Something has already developed."

"Really?" Clare's voice had a tinge of avid curiosity, as it had had when they were girls in the schoolroom, sharing *on-dits* overheard behind the doors of their mother's parties.

Emily remembered Duncan's kiss, in all its shocking, wonderful detail. "Yes. In my studio. He kissed me. And I tried to discourage him. I told him it was too soon after Simon's death. I don't think he believed me, and he was angry." Misery seeped through her as it all came back to her.

"But he isn't angry now?"

Emily shook her head. "We have come to an understanding that we should just be friends. At least, I thought we had." She looked down and stroked the fine silk spangled with gold lace. "I don't want to lose my soul in marriage, just when I have finally found it again."

Clarissa reached for her hand. "Marriage does not always mean subservience. You had a dreadful experience with Simon, but not all men are like him. Matthew does not order me about — I would not stand for it."

"Yes, but I am not you. And Duncan seems eager to bend me to his wishes." She told Clarissa of the episode with Charles Walsh, and Duncan's frequent attempts to get her to hang her paintings downstairs. "He persuades with kindness rather than cruelty, but the results are the same."

"Em, you must not take these things too much to heart. All relationships — between friends, between partners, between siblings — involve give and take. I have seen you grow and change, just in the last little while. You should not fear being able to stand up for yourself."

Emily doubted that. But that was not her most pressing concern. "Clare, even if all that were true, there is something else. It is almost unspeakable."

Clare squeezed her hand. "You can tell me."

Hot tears scalded Emily's cheeks, but

she scarcely noticed them. "Duncan adores children."

"So do you." Clare handed her a linen handkerchief.

"Yes. But Simon and I were married five years and I did not . . ." Emily could not say it.

"You had no children, but I had always assumed that it was because you and Simon did not —"

Emily shook her head violently, willing her sister not to finish the sentence and talk of things that were better left unsaid. "Oh, we did." Her voice was a monotone. "It was not for lack of trying." She hugged her arms about herself as she remembered how Simon would come to her room, night after night, often drunk and almost always in foul humor.

"Did he hurt you, Em?" Clare murmured.

"No. But he made it clear that a woman who cannot bear a child is not worth much as a wife."

There. It was out in the open. Emily felt sick with the effort of saying it.

"That is not true, Em!" Clarissa exclaimed as she gave her sister a quick, fierce hug. "There are many women who cannot have children. Medical facts are no measure of a person's worth."

"But if you could only observe Duncan with his daughter. He dotes on her. Other men might accept a barren wife, but it would gnaw at him." Emily stared at the floor.

"Have you spoken to him of this?"

She shook her head. The miserable tears continued to flow. "How could I? I could barely speak of it to you."

"I think you are wrong not to raise the issue, Em. You cannot know for certain what he thinks."

"He is too kind. He would probably say it is no matter, just to spare my feelings. And, truly, there is no need. As I said, we are just friends now."

"If you are just friends, then there is no reason you cannot try on his gift, is there?" Clare's gaze was steady and her logic impeccable, as always.

Emily wiped her eyes. "You should have been a barrister."

"No, I should have been a mantua maker, because I love pretty clothes. And if you do not try on that gown in the next two minutes, I am going to take it home myself."

Emily lifted the glittering dress from the bed. It would not hurt to put it on just for a minute.

Eleven

"Father, why are you and Grandfather wearing lady's dresses?"

Behind Duncan, Ian McAllister snorted. "Dresses! This is what comes of raising your bairn in England." He knelt on the foyer floor in front of Susannah. "That is nae a dress, lass. 'Tis the McAllister tartan, and 'tis high time your father put it on again."

Even though he knew that the historical accuracy of the "McAllister" tartan could be disputed, and even though their branch of the family had not lived in the Highlands for several generations, Duncan felt his father's reproach was justified. It had been far too long since he had worn Highland dress. Other Scots had fought long to regain the right to wear such clothes, and Duncan had shown a shameful lack of gratitude.

When his mother had first taken the kilt out of her traveling trunk, he had shaken his head. "I cannot wear that now. 'Tis years since I put it on. It will not fit."

"Humor me, Duncan."

215

So of course, he had donned it. And after Libby made a few minor alterations, it fit as it had more than a decade ago, when he had worn it to squire Olivia to *ceilidhs* in the countryside around Edinburgh, just after graduating from Oxford.

He had left his tartan behind when he and Olivia moved to London. There was not much call for Highland dress in Chelsea, and he felt that a man who rarely spoke his native tongue had little right to wear his native clothing.

He remembered Emily saying she loved hearing Scottish words. Would she be as enthralled by Scottish apparel?

He could only hope.

He did like Emily, very much. Now that his business woes were resolved, he hoped she would reciprocate his regard. In time, they could have a good marriage — not the meeting of minds he had shared with Olivia, but that was to be expected. He and his late wife had known each other from childhood and had developed a unique bond.

But just because he would never find another Olivia did not mean he should never remarry. Emily was charming and sweet, and she seemed to enjoy his company.

Perhaps tonight he would overcome her

last objections to his suit. And if a wee touch of Highland glamour aided him in that objective, so be it.

"You are right, Father. It is high time I held up the standard for the London branch of Clan McAllister." He smiled at his father and, to his astonishment, his father smiled back.

"You have been doing that admirably well, son. Ye dinnae need a kilt to accomplish it." With that, Ian turned and shouted up the stairs. "Are ye women going to take all night to primp, or will we get to Lady Tuncliffe's sometime before midnight?"

It had been brief, but Duncan had not heard incorrectly. His father had intimated that he was proud of him.

Life was improving, and no mistake.

Emily's house in Berkeley Square was ablaze with light as Duncan and Penny followed their parents along the pavement. The crush of carriages in the square was heavy, and they had been forced to alight several houses down the street. A light breeze blew the folds of the red and black McAllister tartan about Duncan's knees.

"You look grand, Duncan," Penny said, giving his arm a light squeeze. "A true

Highland laddie."

His mother turned at this comment and smiled. "Our hostess will be astonished to see two such fierce-looking Scots on her doorstep."

"I wonder if she will be wearing your gift?" Penny whispered as Mrs. McAllister turned back toward the house. "If it did not fit, perhaps you will be forced to wear it to Jackson's in the end. You have paid for it, after all. It would be a shame to waste it!"

Duncan smiled at her jest, but his thoughts were elsewhere. He had heard nothing in response to the gift, which he had hired a messenger to deliver that afternoon.

Had he been too presumptuous, and injured Emily's pride once again?

Well, she could hardly throw him out on his ear tonight of all nights, he thought as they climbed the short flight of stairs to her door.

"It was very kind of Lady Tuncliffe to host this gathering," his mother remarked as his father rapped the door knocker. "And I am curious to see the results of your handiwork, Duncan."

His mother's comments distracted him from his worries about Emily. If nothing else, this evening would be an opportunity to show his father that the years in London had not been wasted. Duncan was proud of his designs for Emily's house.

A gray-haired butler whom Duncan remembered from Stonecourt answered the door. Lady Langdon had evidently shared some of her staff with her sister for this grand occasion — a wise decision, he reflected, as the crush of elegantly attired people thronging the small foyer likely would have overwhelmed poor Gertie.

Emily had wanted to host a small supper for the combined McAllister and Denham families and a few friends, followed by the party itself, but Penny had convinced her that she should not attempt too much at once for her first grand occasion in the new house. Because the idea of the supper had been jettisoned, all the guests were arriving at once.

Handing his hat to the butler, Duncan negotiated his way through the milling throng, Penny in tow. He motioned her to precede him up the stairs. "After you, *mamzelle*. After all, you are zee guest of honor, no? It would be rude —"

The rest of the gibe died on his lips as he raised his gaze to the upper story. At the top of the stairs, her back slightly turned to

219

the entrance as she chatted with an elderly female guest, stood Emily.

For bringing him into that dress shop, Duncan owed Penny a very large debt.

Emily's hair had been drawn up into a complicated topknot, with golden ringlets framing her face. Around her throat was a circlet of pearls, with matching bobs in her shell-like ears.

Duncan's attention moved to the gown she wore. In the combination of purplish blue silk and gossamer golden lace, she looked like an angel come to life from a Botticelli painting.

But as he observed how the shimmering fabric clung to her, especially around the daring neckline, his thoughts were anything but cherubic.

She turned back toward the stairs just as he placed his foot on the landing. His mouth was like sawdust.

"Good evening, Emily," he finally managed to say. He leaned over her hand to kiss it, and her delicate violet cologne enveloped him like mist.

"Good evening and welcome," she murmured as he straightened. "You are looking elegant tonight."

"I would say the same to you, except that 'elegant' does not begin to convey how radiant you are."

Dimly, he realized that Penny had evaporated. Gone searching for Rossley, no doubt.

"If I am radiant, it is due to the skill of an excellent mantua maker." She paused. "I attempted several times to write a letter of thanks, but words on paper could not adequately convey my gratitude."

"It was my pleasure to do it. My business is on the mend, and it is all thanks to you."

She smiled, and nearly dazzled him back down the stairs. "From your ensemble, am I to assume that this is the night you will treat me to one or two of Burns's verses?"

"I just might. It feels like a night when anything could happen."

She looked away for a moment, then turned her head back, as though she could not drag her gaze away.

He knew the feeling.

"Do you mean to monopolize Lady Tuncliffe for the entire evening?" his father's voice boomed, shattering the spell between Duncan and Emily. Her wry smile reflected Duncan's thoughts.

"May I request the honor of a dance this evening?" he asked as he moved away.

She bit her lip, then nodded before

turning away to greet his father.

Duncan's step was lighter than it had been in many months as he made his way to the drawing room.

Emily dutifully greeted the elder McAllisters. But, if pressed before a magistrate, she would not have been able to recall a word she said to them.

From the corner of her eye, she watched Duncan's progress down the corridor.

There were easily a dozen gentlemen crammed into the foyer, the stairwell, and the corridor, and just as many women. But Duncan stood out among them all.

It wasn't just the kilt. Rather, it was something in the way he moved — along with the natural grace she had noted before, there was an ease with his surroundings that was new.

He seemed to belong here.

Well, it was not surprising. He had designed this very corridor, after all, helping her select the moldings and paint, and enlarging the window that glowed with the last faint rays of the summer sunset.

"Lady Tuncliffe?"

A guest's hesitant voice alerted her to her fuzzy-mindedness. Flustered, she returned her full attention to the line of people streaming up the staircase.

After what seemed like hours but had been only forty minutes or so, Emily left her post on the landing and moved to the drawing room. Like the other rooms Duncan had redesigned, it was now an airy, pleasing space.

Gone were the heavy brown velvet draperies and faded silk wall hangings that had made the original chamber rather oppressive. In their stead were walls painted a fresh, pale green, with curtains of champagne-colored watered silk. Along with a coat of paint on the ceiling, repairs to one crumbling wall, and some new floorboards, that was all it had taken to transform the room into a gem.

Candles glittered in sconces and along the mantel, lighting pale fires in the diamonds most of the older women wore. Such adult finery had been deemed off limits to Lucy, who nonetheless looked charming in a white frock and their mother's pearls.

"Em, your soirée is already a success!" her sister exclaimed. "I have been introduced to a young gentleman, Mr. Phillips, who is eager to partner me in a country dance. I thought you would never arrive so that we could begin."

Emily smiled at Lucy's impatience, and scanned the room for Penny and Alex. As the guests of honor, it fell to them to begin the dancing. She spotted Penny sipping a glass of ratafia while chatting with Emily's mother, but she could not see Alex.

Twisting around, she finally spied him deep in conversation with Duncan McAllister.

Emily knew she was not an objective judge, but she believed not a man in the room could hold a candle to Duncan in his Highland finery. His fitted black coat with its gleaming silver buttons hugged his shoulders like a second skin, and the red and black tartan was striking.

She had once heard a young dandy sneer at an elderly gentleman strolling down Bond Street in a kilt. "The city streets are no place for a man to make sport in a woman's finery," the fop had drawled to his companion. Fortunately, the dignified old man had not heard the remark.

At the time, Emily had been appalled at the dandy's rudeness. But as she watched Duncan McAllister, another thought also struck her: however one might choose to classify Highland dress, "feminine" was the last word that would spring to mind.

For one thing, those knee-high stockings

showed off a gentleman's strong calves much more vividly than the best tailored pair of pantaloons ever could.

Emily realized she was staring, and quickly turned away. "I will be back in a moment," she told Lucy, crossing the room to speak to Penny.

She sighed. She had known it would be difficult to see Duncan tonight. Her fantasies of waltzing in his arms had danced through her head the previous evening, chasing away sleep for many hours.

But she could not simply flee from him for the rest of her life. They were soon to be related, and the sooner she learned to deal with him in a polite, platonic fashion, the better it would be for everyone. This would simply be a trial by fire.

The dress had made everything more complicated. She knew she should have sent it back, but she could not. The temptation to spend just one night as a belle of the ball — secondary, of course, to Penny and Lucy — had been too great.

Emily finally pushed her way to the corner where Penny was still chatting with Emily's mother, and asked the younger woman to collect Alex.

"What a charming room this is!" Sophia Denham exclaimed as Penny hurried away.

"Your architect friend is to be commended for his fine work."

Emily smiled at her mother. "I am glad that you like it, Mama. And I am so pleased that both you and Papa were able to attend tonight."

"Of course we would come — even your father realizes that certain social niceties cannot be avoided." Sophia's laugh was tinged with bitterness. "But thank you for asking Penny's father to partner me for the first dance. I know it is not precisely traditional, but it will make the evening so much more pleasant for me."

"It seemed the simplest solution," Emily said. "No one will expect Papa to dance after the first set, as it is well known how much he loathes it. He will partner Penny's mother, and then the two of you will be free to do as you wish. I have already ensured that the card tables are ready in the salon, so you will likely not encounter Papa again after the first dance."

"You are an angel, my sweet. As always, you have thought of everything." The marchioness kissed Emily on the cheek and strolled off to find the elder Mr. McAllister.

Emily smiled. Everything was moving according to plan. She crossed the room once more to speak to her old acquaintance Mary Dearborn, who had graciously agreed to provide the music for the evening.

Once they had agreed on the order of the first few pieces and Mary had settled down at the pianoforte, Emily felt a light tap on her shoulder. She turned.

"Have you promised this dance to anyone?" Duncan asked, surveying her with a lazy smile.

She shook her head, not trusting herself to speak.

"Then I am in luck. May I have the honor?" He sketched a small bow.

The first dance? In front of all these people? Emily's heart began to thud dully against her ribcage. She did not know if she could remain calm and poised, even in the intricate steps of the mincing minuet, if she was partnered with Duncan — so familiar, and yet so dashing that she felt she barely knew him.

She nibbled on her bottom lip.

"If you are afraid that you have forgotten the steps, I can simply swing you around in the air like I do Susannah."

Despite her nervousness, she laughed at the image his words painted.

"But the first dance should be just for the families."

"You and I are family — of the happy couple, I mean."

There was no argument against that.

"And since Lucy has been borne off to the refreshment table by some gentleman named Phillips, they cannot serve as fourth couple. I would say our services are required," he added.

She smiled. A minuet would be much safer, after all, than a waltz.

"I would be pleased to accompany you," she said, allowing him to escort her to the middle of the floor and trying not to notice his hand on her elbow.

Mary Dearborn played the first few notes of the familiar minuet they had chosen, and the dancers moved to their places. Emily and Duncan formed a set with her father and Duncan's mother.

"Keeping me separated from the wild lioness for the beginning of the dance, are you, Emily?" Lewis Denham asked, nodding toward the other set, where his estranged wife was chatting amiably with the elder Mr. McAllister.

"I thought it prudent," Emily murmured. Surely her father would not cause a scene tonight, of all nights?

The dancers bowed and curtsied, and Emily placed her hand in Duncan's. His hand felt warm and strong through her thin silk glove. Inside her kid slippers, her toes curled.

"I went to great trouble to remodel this room, and I have no wish to see it reduced to tatters. Lionesses — and lions — can have fearsome claws," Duncan remarked to the Marquess of Wickford as they stepped toward the other couple.

Emily held her breath at Duncan's gibe. Her father was not widely known for his sense of the ridiculous.

To her astonishment, he emitted a dry, rusty laugh. "Touché. Am I to assume that you are Mr. McAllister, Emily's architect?"

"The same, my lord."

"You have done a masterful job."

Mrs. McAllister beamed as they stepped back. "It does look lovely, Duncan."

"Thank you, both."

As the dancers progressed through the formal figures of the minuet, Emily stayed silent, content simply to watch Duncan move.

She longed for a sketchpad as strongly as she had the day she had watched him looking out the windows of her kitchen. Her flights of fancy were improper, but she could no more stop herself from admiring Duncan McAllister than she could halt her own breathing.

At the end of the piece, he returned to her side.

"The next dance will be a quadrille," Emily announced as she curtsied to Duncan and moved away from the dance floor.

"Would you partner me again?" he asked.

"It would be improper to dance together twice in a row," she whispered. "People would talk."

He frowned. "And we cannot have that, can we?"

She recognized that tone of voice. "Not tonight. This is Alex and Penny's night, and Lucy's. I will cause no scandal."

He held up his hands in mock self-defense. "Sheathe your claws! I promise I will do nothing to harm the least of your cubs."

Emily smiled despite herself. "You do say the most ridiculous things."

"Keep a dance for me. Once you have done a proper amount of socializing, I will be back." With that, he strode across the room to speak to his father.

The next few hours flew by for Emily. She checked on Cook's progress in the kitchen, retrieved some sheet music from the salon for Mary Dearborn, danced with Alex, listened to Lucy's breathless litany of Mr. Phillips's attributes, introduced the senior McAllisters to numerous guests, and made sure Gertie replenished the punch at frequent intervals.

She was sitting alone when Mary launched into a waltz.

"Has it been long enough that the arbiters of the *ton* will not be scandalized?" Duncan stood before her, holding out his hand.

Emily quailed as she listened to the music. This was no minuet.

"I will be a perfect gentleman," he said, as if listening to her thoughts. "But you really must dance. All the younger ladies are waiting to follow your lead."

Emily glanced around and saw that Duncan spoke the truth.

She placed her hand in his and allowed him to raise her. "Far be it from me to shirk my duty as hostess." Realizing that she sounded ungracious, she added, "It will be my pleasure."

He led her to the middle of the dance floor then pinned her with a sly look. "Goodness, I have completely forgotten what comes next!" he exclaimed.

She knew some foolishness was afoot.

"Should we sit down then?"

"No, no, wait a minute. I have it!" He raised his arm in a slight curve above his head, as if about to do a Scottish fling. "Is this right?"

Her smile cracked and she burst into laughter. "If you are about to do your impression of ten lords a-leaping, yes."

He lowered his arm and furrowed his brow as if in thought. "But that is not what we are about here, is it?"

Still chuckling, but aware they had to start dancing soon before they attracted attention, Emily moved toward him and placed one hand on his shoulder.

"What are you about, my lady?" he asked in mock shocked tones. "Do you have an ulterior motive in mind, placing your hands on my person?"

Emily stifled memories of the last time her arms had been around Duncan's person. "I will wring your neck, you silly gander, if you do not get serious! We have an assembly to lead."

"Being serious has always been highly overrated, in my opinion," he said, taking up her hand and putting his other hand on her waist. He moved so quickly she was not prepared for the tremor that arced through her body from the point just above her hip where his hand rested.

"Are you ready?" he asked in a low voice.

She nodded.

He said nothing more before spinning her into the music of the dance.

The formal steps of the minuet had not begun to do justice to Duncan's dancing skills. Throughout the waltz, Emily was barely aware of her slippers scuffing the parquet floor. With grace and confidence, he guided her through the elegant movements. The animal grace she had so often noted when he walked was like magic when he danced.

And by dancing with him, she was part of it.

She closed her eyes for just a moment and inhaled the heady aromas of flowers, beeswax, and sweets that filled the room. Under it all, like a sweet major chord at the base of a symphony, was the note of sandalwood and clean, male scent that were Duncan's alone.

If only she was a different person. If only she did not know how much he loved children.

"Resting your eyes, Emily?"

Her eyelids flew open. "Just relaxing."

"I am glad to know that you can find

being in my arms relaxing." His voice held a note she had not heard since that afternoon in her studio.

Suddenly, relaxing was the last idea that came to mind.

"Are you enjoying the party?" she asked, her voice coming out as something closer to a mouse's squeak than to a human sound.

"Very much at the minute."

What had she done, by accepting this dress, by accepting this dance? Had she given him the impression that she was encouraging his suit?

Of course she had, she thought miserably. No matter what her head told her, her heart had barreled ahead all on its own.

The room spun by as they continued to dance. Around and around it went, just like her thoughts.

"Penny tells me that your business has already begun to recover," she said, seizing the first topic that came into her head.

"Yes, it has, thanks to you. I am hopeful that, within six months, I will have fully recovered from Harris's slanderous campaign."

"I am glad to hear it."

"Once my business is back on its feet, I will be much more ready to pursue other interests." His last two words melted over her like chocolate.

"Other interests?" The squeak had returned.

"Yes. Such as — oh, I don't know — archery, I suppose. Or collecting snuff boxes."

Emily's laughter erupted like a pent-up sneeze. It was so loud, in fact, that several other dancers turned to look at her.

"You laugh at my choice of amusements?"

"I laugh because you are so preposterous!" And out of sheer relief that the intensity in his voice had evaporated.

He frowned. "Preposterous? You slight me. You are lucky I did not bring my ceremonial sword!"

"You have a ceremonial sword?"

"Not really. But I could hide a small dagger in my sporran, I suppose."

"What is a sporran?"

He nodded downward. "That thing about my waist that looks like a wild man's pelt. It is a bag that shepherds once wore to carry their food to the fields. Perhaps I should get Susannah one for biscuits."

For the rest of the dance, he amused her with historical tidbits about Highland dress, and her breath stopped coming in short, sharp bursts.

But as he escorted her from the dance floor, Duncan leaned down and whispered in her ear, in a voice so soft that she almost could not hear it: "The waltz is such an intimate dance. Almost as enjoyable as kissing, would you not agree?"

Before she could marshal her wits to reply, he had bowed to her and departed, with one last devilish smile and a whirl of tartan.

Dazed, she stood motionless at the side of the room for a moment or two before hurrying to the kitchen to check on Cook. And although the party continued until the early morning hours, she was careful not to find herself alone with Duncan again.

Heaven only knew what he would say next.

Twelve

Emily had tried but she could not sleep.

After tossing and turning for the better part of an hour, she crawled out of bed, lit a small branch of candles on her bedside table, and tried to concentrate on a novel she had recently borrowed from Hatchard's circulating library.

Even the complicated yarn of an orphan girl, her guardian, and a malicious squire could not keep Emily's attention long, however.

It was two nights after Alex and Penny's betrothal party. The first evening, exhausted from the festivities, Emily had tumbled into bed and slept the sleep of the dead. To her embarrassment, she had slept so late that she had even missed a visit from Duncan's parents, who had stopped by to say thank you and good-bye on their way out of Town. They were off to the country to visit friends for a few weeks, but would return for Alex and Penny's wedding in a month.

It must have been her odd sleeping pattern the day before that kept her so wakeful now, she thought. Although the fact that she could not stop reliving her waltz with Duncan was not helping.

A pounding at the front door disrupted her thoughts.

She glanced at the small silver clock on the mantel. It was almost one in the morning.

"Who on earth could that be?" she wondered aloud, hastily donning a wrapper and warm felt slippers, and seizing the branch of candles. She did not intend to reveal herself, but she was curious to hear who was calling. Pausing on the landing, she heard Gertie open the front door.

"I'm so sorry to rouse you at this hour, but I must see Lady Tuncliffe immediately!" Penny's panicked voice echoed in the empty foyer.

"But Miss McAllister, it's very late," the housemaid began.

"It is all right, Gertie, I am awake." Emily ran down the stairs two at a time. Had something happened to Duncan or Susannah?

She wished fervently that Alex were here, but he was out with friends trolling the clubs of St. James's.

"Penny!" she cried on seeing the

238

younger woman's ashen face. "What has happened?"

"It's Susannah," Penny gasped. "She is desperately ill with some sort of fever. The doctor is there now, but Duncan is out of his mind with worry and I cannae seem to calm him."

Emily gripped the oak banister for support. Fevers could be swift and terrible killers, as Duncan knew all too well. No wonder he was distraught.

"Is Susannah's nurse there?" Surely Nurse would know about childhood fevers.

Penny shook her head. "She's gone to Gloucestershire for her brother's wedding, and she's not expected back for a week. Please come, Emily!"

"I will come, of course," Emily replied. "But I do not know what help I will be." Even as she said it, she remembered the dark days a decade ago, when her sister Lucy had been touched by just such an illness. Then, all Emily had been able to do was beg to help, as older people bustled about and paid her little heed.

"I think your presence alone will calm Duncan."

As Emily ran up the stairs to dress, she wondered whether that was true. But if Penny thought she could help, she would do her utmost to be of service.

The two women said little during the short ride in the McAllisters' curricle through dark, deserted streets. Somewhere in the distance, Emily heard a clock tower bell pealing. That and the clopping of the horses' hooves were the only sounds.

As soon as the carriage drew to a halt, they stumbled out, ran up the stairs, and rushed into the familiar foyer. There, they almost tumbled over Libby, who had been pacing the hall awaiting their arrival.

"Thank heavens you're back, Miss McAllister. And it's so good that you're here, Lady Tuncliffe. Mr. McAllister has been almost frantic since Dr. Kerr left."

Penny led the way up two narrow flights of stairs to Susannah's chamber. It was a plain and pleasant room, with a large window overlooking the garden. A small rag doll was propped on the sill.

Emily's gaze moved to the corner occupied by a small iron bedstead. Next to it on a wooden chair, illuminated by a single candle, sat Duncan.

She would hardly have known him as the dashing man who had squired her about the dance floor just two nights ago. His face was taut and dusted with stubble, and his cuffs hung open. He was stroking his daughter's flushed face. Susannah was asleep, a sheen of perspiration on her forehead.

"The doctor gave her a sleeping draft," Duncan explained in a hushed monotone. "There is little he can do until he is certain what she has." He paused. "Kerr suspects it is rheumatic fever."

Emily stifled a gasp.

"What symptoms does he expect to appear? Did he say?"

"If her joints begin to swell, it is likely rheumatic fever. A wracking cough with blood could mean pneumonia." Duncan's voice was devoid of expression.

"Is there anything we can do in the meantime?" Emily asked, feeling for all the world like a hapless fifteen-year-old again.

Duncan lifted dull eyes to her face. "Please, just stay."

"I will stay as long as you like." Emily struggled to speak against the lump that had formed in her throat.

As she settled onto a chair that Libby had dragged from an adjoining bedroom, Emily shivered, although the night was warm. Almost as terrifying as the sight of the small, perspiring child was the sight of Duncan — normally so lighthearted — twisting a corner of Susannah's bedclothes in fruitless agitation.

Penny took a seat on the divan, and no one spoke. The only sound came from the bed, as Susannah occasionally grizzled in her sleep.

Emily wished with all her heart there was something she could do to comfort Duncan and Penny. But she was not a magician. All she could do was wait with them.

Hours later, a shriek shook Emily from her light slumber.

Wildly, she looked about the unfamiliar room, almost tumbling off her chair. Where was she? Who had cried out?

"It's all right, bairn," she heard Duncan's murmur, a note of fear just barely detectable in his familiar baritone. "Father's here."

In the circle of lamplight next to Susannah's bed, Duncan was stroking his daughter's forehead as the child thrashed to and fro.

"I'm so hot!" she sobbed. "And itchy!"

Emily stood and hurried toward the bed.

Penny came into the room with a damp cloth, which she laid on her niece's forehead. Susannah shook it off as a low moan wracked her tiny frame.

"Father, I feel so bad!" Her blue eyes were enormous in her red face.

Emily stood at the foot of the bed, in the shadows. As Penny moved back, the candlelight illuminated Susannah more clearly, and Emily thought she saw something at the base of the child's throat.

Something she did not want to see.

She walked around the bed and moved behind Duncan. "May I?" she asked, taking hold of the candlestick. He nodded.

Emily held the light directly over Susannah. The child squeezed her eyes tightly closed.

"There," Emily said, dread tightening around her heart. She pointed to a faint spot just above the neckline of Susannah's lawn nightgown.

Duncan looked.

"That red mark?" His voice was muted.

Emily nodded. "I am no doctor, but —" She stopped. She could not bring herself to say the words.

"Do you recognize it? Believe me, Emily, I am all ears for any sort of opinion. What do you suspect?"

There was nothing to be gained by hiding from the facts. "Scarlet fever," she murmured.

At the words, Duncan's mouth hardened

into a grim line. He looked away, staring out the window into the slowly lightening dawn.

"My sister Lucy had a very light touch of it when she was a few years older than Susannah. It was actually a milder form of the disease, called scarlatina," Emily explained, all the terrible memories rushing back. She remembered her mother's wailing and her father's angry words with the doctor.

"As I was the oldest, I was the only sibling allowed into the sick room. At first, our doctor did not know what she had, until the spots appeared."

"But Lucy recovered." Duncan's voice was devoid of expression. It was as though he did not dare to hope.

"Yes. And if it is scarlet fever, we must work to bring her fever down immediately." Emily remembered the cold cloths, the ices from the confectioner's, the windows open to the crisp fall breeze. Unfortunately, it was summer now, but the early morning air might still be refreshing. She ran to the window and raised the sash. Blue satin drapes billowed into the room.

"What can I do?" Duncan stood.

Suddenly, Emily stopped moving.

"What if I am wrong?" she whispered.

The question hung in the air unanswered.

"What if you are right?" Penny piped up from the corner.

Duncan nodded. "Aye. The doctor could nae say what the fever was, either, and we will nae be able to get him here for an hour at least. It cannae hurt to keep Susannah cool in the interim. And it may help."

Emily noted how pronounced Duncan's burr had become, and how often Scots expressions crept into his speech. His terror was close to the surface, she realized.

"I will fetch Dr. Kerr." Penny slipped quietly from the room. Moments after she left, Libby rushed in.

"Miss McAllister said you needed to keep Miss Susannah cool," she said in a breathless rush. "My brother works in one of the warehouses at the wharf, where there's an icehouse. Shall I send one of the stable boys with a wagon?"

Duncan nodded. "Thank you, Libby." He withdrew a handful of coins from the pocket of his coat, which he had long ago discarded on a chair. "Give these to the boy. For the ice."

Libby was gone as quickly as she had come, promising to return within minutes with cool water and cloths.

Suddenly, it was just Duncan and Emily, alone with the restless child.

"I pray to God that we are doing the right thing," Emily said.

"At least we are doing something. I thought I was going to go mad, just watching her."

"We are doing all we can do," she whispered.

"I could tickle her and tell her stories," he said. "But I doubt that would be useful."

Libby bustled back into the room, lugging a large pail of water. "It is as cool as we could get it," she said, setting it on the floor. "Drew it from the cistern myself."

Behind her came a young housemaid carrying a pile of linens, which she laid on the divan. Libby sent her back to the cellar for more water and a small washtub.

"Mind the water's cool!" she called after the girl. "This isn't a regular bath."

Emily dipped a cloth in the pail, squeezed it until it was almost dry, moved to the bedside, and drew back the bed's thin counterpane. "Now, this is going to be wet, Susannah," she murmured as the child's eyes flew open. "But you must be a brave little girl. Can you be brave for me?"

Susannah nodded.

She laid the damp towel over Susannah's right arm. The little girl shivered. "Aaaah!" she cried, trying to pluck the offending object away.

"No, Susannah, this will make you feel better. Just lie still."

The child looked up to her father for support, but Duncan shook his head. "Do as Lady Tuncliffe says, bairn."

Susannah lay back against the pillows, and a tear rolled down her flushed cheek. "My throat hurts, Father. It's hard to swallow."

Duncan looked at Emily. She nodded. A sore throat was another sign of scarlet fever.

She passed several cloths to Duncan, who applied them to Susannah's legs and feet. The child squirmed as the wet linen touched her bare skin.

"Father, I don't like the towels!" She was sobbing in earnest now.

"I know, bairn. I know. But it will help. I promise," Duncan said.

"Shhh, Susannah," Emily murmured. "Remember our song?"

The little girl gave no indication that she had heard. She was too focused on trying to shake off the cold cloth that Emily had placed on her neck. Duncan held both of his daughter's hands and murmured soothing nonsense words to her.

"Remember our song?" Emily tried again.

" 'As William and Mary walked by the seaside,' " she sang. " 'Their last farewell to take —' "

Susannah's sobs started to subside.

" 'Should you never return, young William, she said, my poor heart shall surely break.' "

It was not the most cheerful song, at least in its early verses, but it was the only thing Emily could think of to calm the child. The pretty tune had always helped Susannah focus on Emily during their painting sessions, rather than on the birds outside the window.

"My stomach hurts," Susannah whimpered.

"We're right here, bairn," her father said. "We won't let anything hurt you."

" 'Be not thus dismayed, young William, he said, as he pressed the young maid to his side,' " Emily continued.

Duncan replaced the damp cloth, smoothing it over the child's forehead. This time, Susannah let it be.

"I'm so hot," she murmured, and hiccupped. She lay back down on the bed and closed her eyes.

" 'Nor my absence mourn, for when I return, I will make little Mary my bride.' "

Susannah subsided into silence. The two adults exchanged glances over the tiny bed.

"I did not know you possessed such a sweet singing voice, Emily," Duncan whispered.

"It was the only thing I could think of," Emily replied. "I wish I knew more of children's illnesses!"

"As do I. She has always been such a sturdy wee bairn. She rarely even sneezes."

Emily's heart went out to him. With his neckcloth loose around the open collar of his shirt, and plain felt slippers on his feet, he looked vulnerable and lost. She longed to embrace him, even as she realized how improper that would be.

Suddenly, she felt like an intruder.

"Are you certain you want me here?" she asked, moving toward the door. "Susannah seems quiet now, and the doctor will be here soon. If you would like some privacy, I can go."

"No, please stay," Duncan said. His intense gaze made her long to look away, and yet she could not.

Of course she could not leave.

Thirteen

Duncan took a deep breath as he watched his daughter toss fretfully in the dawn light. Would Penny and the doctor never arrive?

Despite her ginger hair, Susannah looked so like her mother right now. Or perhaps it was just that Duncan's last memory of Olivia also involved dim rooms, rumpled bedclothes, and a curious hush.

She could not die. He would not let it happen.

Of course, he had said the same thing at Livvy's bedside, and she had slipped from him nonetheless.

Susannah stirred. "May I have some water?" she whispered.

"Of course, bairn." He poured her a glass from the pitcher on the windowsill. The water was lukewarm; Libby had boiled it first, as the doctor had ordered.

As his daughter opened her mouth to drink, he noted that her tongue was whitish. He gestured to Emily, who was sitting on the divan sipping a cup of tea. As she walked over to the bed, he pointed toward his tongue, then to the child.

Susannah handed the water glass back to Duncan.

"Can you yawn for Lady Tuncliffe? A big yawn?"

Obediently, the child stretched her mouth open. Emily looked inside, then nodded to Duncan. "I remember Lucy looked the same," she whispered.

He laid his hand on Susannah's forehead, and almost flinched. She was burning with fever.

"Should we get her into the bath?" he asked. Libby and the housemaid had brought the tub into Susannah's room, and filled it with cool water. Emily nodded.

Together, they removed the child's nightgown, then Duncan carried her to the tub.

"It isn't bath night," Susannah mumbled sleepily. "I had my bath last week."

"This is a special bath," he murmured, lowering her into the shallow water.

"It's cold!" she howled, gripping the sides of the tub and starting to cry. "Libby forgot the hot water!"

"But you said you were warm," Duncan replied, wondering briefly why he thought reasoning would work with a three-year-old child.

"I'm not! I'm cold!" Susannah cried.

251

" 'As William and Mary walked by the seaside, their last farewell to take . . .' "

His voice was tentative. He had not sung a note since forced to do so during morning services by an unpleasant master at Harrow. His voice was rusty.

" 'If you don't come back —' "

"That's not the words, Father!" Susannah wailed.

"I need help," he said. "How do the words go?"

"I don't remember." Susannah's voice was mulish.

" 'Should you never return, young William, she said, my poor heart shall surely break.' " Emily's voice was clear and sweet.

" 'Be not thus dismayed, young William said.' " This time, Susannah's and Emily's voices rose together.

"Are you not going to join in?" Emily asked him with a smile.

"I am afraid my talents lie in other directions."

"We are a very forgiving audience. Well, at least I am, and Susannah will learn to be."

"Nae, I prefer to listen." He settled back on his heels and watched as Emily scooped water over the little girl's back.

She was very natural with Susannah, as

though she had been used to raising children all her life. He supposed, as an elder sister, she had been no stranger to little ones. And when she had been painting the portrait, she had seemed to enjoy spending time with Susannah.

So why had she had no children of her own? Had she been unable? Had Simon been impotent? Or had she and Simon spent so little time together that they had not had the opportunity to . . .

He halted that train of thought. Such matters were none of his affair.

Emily finished bathing the child, then wrapped her in a towel. Duncan scooped Susannah up and laid her back on the bed.

Despite the cool breeze and the drops of water beading her skin, the child was still flushed. But her eyelids were drooping.

Emily sang her another short song, and within minutes she had drifted back to sleep.

"Where is Dr. Kerr?" Duncan muttered, pulling out his pocket watch. "He should have been here long ago."

"It seems as though Penny has been gone a long while, but it is scarcely more than half an hour since she left," Emily observed.

"You are right. I am simply impatient."

Emily drew in a sharp breath, released it, started to speak, stopped.

"You must not be afraid to say anything to me," Duncan said. "I would rather know the truth than hide from it."

Emily stared at the floor for a moment, then raised her head. "If things progress as they did for Lucy, the next few days will tell the tale. Either the symptoms will quickly fade, or . . ." She left the thought unfinished.

Duncan nodded, unable to speak.

Susannah was the light of his life. There had been days, in the weeks after Olivia's death, when his daughter had been the only reason he had found the strength to get out of bed.

Despite his best efforts, an iron band of panic began to press against his chest, and his head began to buzz. He breathed in slowly, deeply.

The dizziness receded.

Emily reached out and seized his hand between both of hers. She rubbed it, and only then did he realize that his skin was ice cold. Her touch was like balm on an open wound.

What would he do without this calm, compassionate woman? If anything happened to her, he would be as desolate as he was now at Susannah's bedside.

The thought struck him as harshly as the cold bath had struck his daughter. His mind began to spin again, and the dizziness hovered on the edge of his consciousness.

"Duncan? Are you all right?"

He withdrew his hand from hers.

"Aye, just distracted. But you look tired. Why dinnae you lie down on the divan? Susannah will likely stay calm now until the doctor arrives."

"I doubt I will be able to sleep."

"Of course, if you prefer the guest room, I can have Libby prepare it." He stood and headed for the door, but Emily shook her head.

"No, that is all right. I will stay here, if you do not mind." She walked away and curled up on the divan, and he returned to his post next to Susannah's bed.

He should have insisted that Emily sleep in a proper bed. But, he admitted to himself, he needed her here.

At the thought, he shivered. He had promised himself that he would never need another woman again. But it was clear that he had been fooling himself and behaving most dishonorably to Emily — pretending that what they shared was light and harmless. He should have pulled back after that day in her studio.

There was still time, he reassured himself as he watched her sleep. Even during the betrothal party, he had sensed that she still had reservations about him. If he dropped his pursuit now, they would both escape relatively unscathed.

Duncan rubbed his temples. How could he have been so blind? Without meaning to, without wanting to — without even realizing he was capable of doing so — he had fallen in love with Emily Wallace.

What monumental folly. The more people one loved, the more open one was to despair.

Duncan stroked his daughter's hair and willed the doctor to arrive.

Despite Duncan's entreaties, Emily had not been able to sleep. Instead, she lay quietly under the light coverlet Libby had provided.

It had taken her some time to shake the feeling that it was improper for her to be in this chamber alone with Duncan. But then she remembered that she was a widowed woman now — and much more latitude was given to widows than to green, young girls.

She was glad of it. She would not have foregone the opportunity to help, no matter what the foolish rules of propriety. Duncan had given her that — the confidence to look past the rules of the *ton*, in painting or in anything else.

Through half-closed eyes, she watched him as he paced the floor beside his daughter's bed. Then he stopped, and leaned over to brush a curl from Susannah's cheek.

The tenderness of the gesture wrenched Emily's heart. How she had wanted to share such a bond with a child.

At that moment, she heard steps in the corridor. The door opened, and Penny entered the room with a gray-haired gentleman.

"Dr. Kerr." Duncan came toward him. "Sorry to have roused you."

"Do not apologize, Mr. McAllister," the doctor answered in a thick Yorkshire accent. "It is part of my job. Your sister says you suspect scarlet fever?"

"Yes," Emily interjected. "I could be wrong, but the symptoms are very like my sister's when she had scarlatina."

"This is Lady Tuncliffe, a friend of the family," Duncan explained.

"What have you observed?" he asked as

he moved to the bedside. Emily listed the telltale signs.

After a short examination, the doctor straightened up. "I believe you are correct, Lady Tuncliffe."

The color began to drain from Duncan's face. Once again, Emily longed to embrace him.

"You and Mr. McAllister were very wise to apply cold water. The case, at the moment, seems to be a mild one. If you can continue to keep her fever in check, there is a chance that the illness will pass quickly."

Penny shot a quick, hopeful look at her brother. The doctor caught it, and frowned.

"I can make no promises," he warned. "And I will visit this afternoon to examine her again. All we can do is hope for the best."

"I understand." Duncan's voice was lifeless as he escorted the doctor to the door.

The days and nights that followed Dr. Kerr's visit passed in a continuous, indistinguishable stream. Emily, Duncan, and Penny took turns at Susannah's bedside, often in pairs while the third person slept. Alex was dispatched to the country to share the sad news with the senior McAllisters and accompany them back to London. Libby and the other servants scurried in and out constantly with towels, water, and bowls of soup. The soup was mainly for the adults; it was almost impossible to convince Susannah to eat, as every mouthful hurt to swallow and agitated her stomach.

One morning it rained, and Emily and Duncan listened in silence to the patter of drops on the roof.

Early one evening, as dusk crept through the window, Duncan overheard Penny murmuring a line from the Twenty-third Psalm over and over as she bathed Susannah's forehead. Tears dropped unheeded onto the soft white rags in Penny's hands.

And very late one night, while Penny had retired to her own room and Emily was sleeping on the divan, he hovered over Susannah's bedside. He brushed a ginger curl from the child's cheek. She was still scorching to the touch.

"I am so sorry I failed you, bairn," he whispered.

"How have you failed her?" Emily's voice startled him as it cut through the gloom.

"I thought you were sleeping."

"I was." She crossed the room into the circle of candlelight. Her hair was disheveled and her face creased with sleep. "What do you mean, you have failed Susannah? No father could have been more devoted than you have been."

Duncan sighed. It was kind of Emily to try to console him, but she did not understand.

"I shouldn't have allowed her to go to the park last week, that day when she looked so peaked. She probably contracted the fever that afternoon. There are always dozens of children in that park. Any one of them could have given it to her." If only he had not been so caught up in his business, in trying to impress his father, in trying to impress Emily.

"Duncan, even the doctors do not know where this fever comes from. My mother said similar things when Lucy fell ill, and the doctor assured her that this disease cannot be prevented. If it could be, do you think so many thousands of children would fall prey to it?"

Duncan refused to be seduced by her easy rationalization. "But I should have kept her indoors."

"You could not keep the child indoors

260

for the rest of her life. She needs sunshine and air to thrive."

"Perhaps that is it." Duncan grasped at anything that could explain why this hideous illness had befallen his daughter. "If we had lived in the country, somewhere more healthful, this might not have happened." He stood up and began to pace.

Emily caught up to him and laid a hand on his arm. "Duncan, stop. Think about it. Children in rural villages and on farms get scarlatina, too. Country air is not a cure for everything. Did you not say that you were in Shropshire when your wife —"

Duncan wrenched his arm from her grasp. "Do not mention Olivia."

Emily's face was stricken. "I am so sorry. That was thoughtless."

Duncan barely heard her apology. He had already moved away from her, toward the window. He slung his forearm across the cool, dark glass, and leaned his forehead against it.

"Duncan, please forgive me." He could barely hear Emily's voice through the rushing noise that filled his ears.

This room was all too similar to the room in that country inn where Livvy had slipped away from him. He had done everything — found doctors, bought medicines, prayed, raged. Nothing had worked. Nothing.

And it was going to happen again.

"What is the use?" he mumbled against his forearm.

"The use of what?" Emily's voice, beside him, was so soft he could barely hear it.

"The use of loving anyone? Olivia — I loved her, but it dinnae do any good! And now Susannah." He stopped, and bit his lower lip until the bitter taste of blood filled his mouth.

"Tell me."

He shook his head.

"I told you about Simon, and it made me feel better."

"This is different."

"Yes, because you loved Olivia, and I did not love Simon. But it helps to share your burdens."

He shook his head again.

To his astonishment, he felt her small hands on his shoulders, kneading the tense muscles through the thin lawn of his shirt.

He sighed as her hands relaxed him. But soon he turned to her.

"I could not stop Livvy from dying. And if Susannah goes, I don't know what I will do."

"Her condition is stable. You shouldn't borrow trouble."

"I cannae help it. If Susannah dies —"

"You will weep and you will mourn, but you will survive. You are tougher than you suspect."

He shook his head. "You have been right about many things, Emily, but this time you are wrong."

Four nights after Susannah's illness had begun, Emily entered the room after a short nap. Duncan beckoned her to the bedside.

"Feel her forehead," he whispered, hope in every syllable.

Emily prayed that she would feel what Duncan so clearly thought he had.

She laid the back of her hand on Susannah's brow. For the first time since she had arrived in the sickroom, the child's skin was almost cool. And the red welts along her throat seemed to be fading.

Exultant, she looked up at Duncan. "I think the fever has broken," she said.

An hour later, Susannah awoke and asked for a biscuit.

"I have never been so happy to give you a sweet in my life," Duncan exclaimed, dashing from the room to procure the treat from the kitchen himself.

Emily smiled as she watched him go.

Closing up his medical bag, Dr. Kerr pronounced Susannah on the mend.

"She will not be quite herself for a week at least," he said as he put his coat back on. "It was a very close call, and she will need time to recover."

Duncan nodded. "But she will recover?"

"As far as I can tell, yes."

"Thank you, Dr. Kerr," Duncan said, shaking the older gentleman's hand. "I cannot tell you how happy I am to hear this news."

"Do not thank me," the physician replied. "I did precious little. With scarlet fever, one can only try to bring down the fever, and pray. I think the quick action you took at the beginning of her illness played just as much of a part in her recovery as anything I did."

At this, Duncan smiled at Emily.

"Do let me know if her condition changes," Dr. Kerr said as he left the sickroom. "I expect it will remain good, however. And don't worry about walking me to the door. I will see myself out."

Duncan, Emily, and Penny listened in silence as the doctor's footsteps faded away along the corridor. Slowly, Penny rose and crossed the room to Susannah's bedside.

"She is beginning to regain her normal color already," Penny said. "And the spots are much less prominent than they were even a few hours ago."

"Thank heaven," Emily said. "Her illness has progressed just as Lucy's did — with the same fortuitous result." Stiffly, she rose from the divan, on which she had slept for a few hours the previous night. "And now that all is well, I believe it is time for me to leave. You will want some private time with Susannah when she awakes, and doubtless you will also want some time to yourselves without the need to amuse a guest."

"I would hardly call you a guest after all you have gone through with us these past few days," Penny said. "You feel more like a sister to me — as you soon will be in reality."

Emily crossed the room and enveloped the younger woman in a gentle embrace. "I am pleased that we will be sisters. And now that Susannah is on the mend, we must return to making plans for your wedding." She glanced over at Duncan. His eyes were sunken in his drawn face, but he had lost the dreadful pallor that had marked him since the day Susannah first took sick.

"You must rest," she said to him, touching his arm. "I doubt you have slept more than a few hours in the past week."

"Don't worry," he replied. "I will go straight to my bed."

Emily nodded. She gathered up the few things she had asked her servants to send over — a change of clothing, a brush, some handkerchiefs — and replaced them in her small traveling bag.

"Goodbye, Susannah," she whispered to the child as she left. "Be good, and get well."

Duncan and Emily descended the staircase in silence. Now that the crisis had passed, a brittle atmosphere seemed to surround them. When Emily's hand accidentally brushed against Duncan's, they leaped apart as if they had been struck.

When they reached the foyer, Duncan summoned Libby and asked her to ensure that his curricle was brought round to convey Lady Tuncliffe home.

"Yes, sir. And then shall I go up and stay with Miss Susannah, so that you and Miss McAllister may rest?"

Duncan nodded, and the maid withdrew.

They stood stiffly in the foyer. The first light of dawn was just beginning to seep through the transom above the door.

"Emily, I cannot thank you enough," Duncan began, but Emily held up her hand. She knew that any expression of gratitude would reduce her to tears.

The anguish, fear, and longing of the past days seemed to pool in her stomach. Over the course of Susannah's illness, she had grown closer to Duncan than to any man she had ever known.

She loved him.

And loving him, she knew that she could never be his wife. He adored children, and Susannah deserved siblings. He felt he had to control his world, and Emily needed freedom.

A marriage between them would be a disaster.

"It was my pleasure to help, Duncan," she said. Impulsively, she reached for his hand and squeezed it.

At her touch, Duncan closed his eyes. He squeezed her hand in return.

"Emily . . . I shouldn't, but I cannae help myself." Without another word, he pulled her into his arms.

Before she could breathe, his lips were on hers. It was not a gentle kiss, nor a fierce one. If anything, he seemed to be seeking something — strength, support, deliverance.

Whatever it was, she needed it in equal measure. Emily kissed him back with an abandon she had never felt in all her six and twenty years.

Kissing Duncan was as wonderful as she had remembered. She breathed in deeply. His mere presence assaulted all her senses. She might have been standing in the middle of Bond Street, for all she was aware of her surroundings.

Emily stood on tiptoe in an effort to get closer to him. Without thought, without reason, she ran her hand down his neck and inside the open collar of his shirt. She could feel his pulse throbbing dully at the base of his throat.

He groaned. Without a word, he broke the kiss, placed his arm behind her knees, and lifted her as though she weighed as little as Susannah. He carried her up the stairs and into the sitting room, and nudged the door closed with the toe of his slipper.

Fourteen

This was wrong. Very wrong. Emily knew it, and still she did not have the will to call a halt.

Duncan laid her down on the familiar sofa, then sat on the floor beside her.

"I shouldn't do this," he murmured. Before she could reply, he kissed her again.

Within moments, her hair had tumbled down around her shoulders. He ran his hands through its length.

"You should always wear your hair this way," he said, chuckling. "You look like a mythological maiden."

"But I am real, and I am no maiden."

As she said the words, she quailed. It was true, she was not an innocent. But her encounters with Simon had had none of the heat and intensity that this embrace foretold.

Duncan seemed to take encouragement from her words. He rained kisses on her forehead, her cheeks, her earlobes, her throat.

"Do you have any idea how you have haunted my dreams, lass?" he murmured

269

as he pushed aside the edge of her gown so he could kiss her shoulder.

"Mmmm," she replied, thinking of the times she had fallen asleep at night thinking of ginger hair and large, capable hands.

Those hands were working magic now. When he moved them to the high, gathered waist of her dress, she stiffened.

"Do not run away this time," he said, his eyes dark in the dim dawn light. "I will not hurt you, I promise."

Emily forced herself to relax. She would never marry again, and so this might be as close as she would ever come to discovering the true nature of the relationship between men and women — something she had never known with Simon.

She knew it was wrong, but she nodded.

He moved his hands higher above her high waist, and it was as though his fingertips were hot fire irons. A low groan escaped her.

"I knew there were depths of passion in you," Duncan murmured.

A knock on the front door sliced through Emily's consciousness like a bullet.

"The coachman!" she cried, sitting bolt upright and accidentally clipping Duncan in the jaw with her arm. He tumbled backward in a manner that might have been comical, had the situation not been so dire.

Duncan seemed to realize the gravity of their position at the same time she did. "Emily, I am so sorry," he began.

"Don't be sorry," she said. "I am not."

They stared at each other.

"But this cannot happen," she added.

He looked away. "I don't know your reasons, but I have my own. And you are right."

The knock on the door was louder this time.

"I will answer it," Duncan said, heaving himself up from the floor. He opened the sitting room door slightly, slipped through it, and closed it behind him.

When he returned moments later, Emily had adjusted her dress. Her hair, she had decided, would have to wait. The coachman would have to make of it what he would.

"I told him you would be out shortly."

Emily nodded. "Duncan, if it could be anyone, it would be you. But I can't."

"I know. I cannae either."

The soft Scots expression almost undid her. This was paining Duncan as much as it pained her. "I think it best if we do not see each other for a while," she said.

Duncan raised his eyebrows. "Is that not somewhat extreme? You can trust me, you know. I will not try to ravish you in the middle of my sitting room in the broad light of day."

His attempt at lightness only added to her misery. "I know. But the problem is, I would be waiting — and hoping that you would try."

"What is it, Emily? What makes you hold back?"

It would be so easy to share her sorrow with him now. But it would solve nothing, and it would hurt too much.

"It is too long a story for the present. Perhaps when we are more rested, and more ourselves. But what about you? Is it Olivia?"

He nodded. "In a way, but not the way you probably think."

Emily stood. "In time, I think we can move past this. But for now, I need to sleep and I need to think."

Duncan nodded. "Aye. So do I."

"So I will make myself scarce for a few weeks. I hope you don't mind."

"I understand."

She reached for his hand. Then, remembering that a similar gesture had launched their passion just moments before, she let her arm drop.

"Good-bye, Duncan. Take care of yourself, and Susannah, and Penny."

"And you be good to yourself. It is unfortunate that your brother has pursued my parents to the country. I wish you were not going home to an empty house."

"I will be fine. Please do not worry. Alex should be back with your parents tonight, and fortunately they will have good news awaiting them."

There was nothing more to say. Emily smoothed down her skirt and walked out the door.

Not turning back was the hardest thing she had ever done.

A few hours later, Penny wandered into the sitting room, yawning. "You are up and about early, Duncan," she said, then stopped. "Heavens, did you not go to bed?"

Duncan knew he must look a fright. After Emily had left, he had paced back and forth in the sitting room, unable to settle, unwilling to go to bed. Finally, in exhaustion, he had collapsed on the sofa.

His mouth felt as though it were full of raw cotton, and his eyes ached. Rubbing his hand over his jaw, he felt a thicket of stubble.

The room smelled faintly of violet perfume.

"Is Susannah awake?" he asked.

"Not yet. I think she's exhausted, poor bairn."

"I should go check on her," Duncan said, rising to his feet.

"She is fine, truly, Duncan. But you look as though you've just come back from the wars."

Duncan sighed.

"Did you have words with Emily?"

"How did you know?"

"Sisterly intuition. What happened?"

"I am not really certain," Duncan confessed as he sank back into the cushions of the sofa. "We have both developed a strong attachment to each other."

"This will not be news to any but the blind."

His smile was weak. "But she is holding back for some reason she will not explain."

"Perhaps it is too soon after the death of her husband?"

"That was a concern for a while, but I do not think it is any longer. Theirs was not a love match, in any case. Something else is bothering her."

"And you?" Penny's voice was gentle.

"I? I will not marry again."

"Olivia would want you to. I know she would want you to be happy."

"It is not that." Duncan did not feel comfortable explaining his fears, even to his sister. What grown man could not face the thought of loving, for fear of losing the loved one? "It is . . . complicated. And since Emily has concerns of her own, it is no matter."

"It pains me to see the two of you so determined to thwart your own happiness."

Duncan wandered over to the fireplace, then poked idly at the smoldering coals that Libby had lit several hours ago. "I am not unhappy. Far from it, now that Susannah is going to recover."

"You look unhappy."

"I am just tired."

As he said it, though, his mind revolved back to the question that had perplexed him all morning. What was Emily's secret?

Methodically, he examined everything he knew about her. She loved her independence. Did she fear he would threaten that? Possibly — she had reacted with heat on the few occasions when he had meddled in her painting affairs.

But there was something deeper than

that. He had seen it in her eyes.

He shook his head. He must stop obsessing about Emily if he was ever to create any distance between them.

At that moment, Libby walked into the sitting room, carrying a letter. "Oh, good, you're awake, Mr. McAllister."

"More or less, Libby."

"A messenger just delivered this. Said it was urgent, but he didn't wait for a reply."

Duncan looked at his sister, but she shook her head. "I am not expecting anything."

He moved to the desk and picked up a letter opener, slit the sealing wax and unfolded the single sheet of paper.

McAllister,

Since you have ignored the message I sent three days ago, I have had no choice but to approach your "friend," Lady Tuncliffe, to ask her to intercede for me on your behalf. A desperate man takes desperate measures.

Harris

What message? What measures?

He had not even looked at his desk since Susannah had fallen ill four days ago.

He handed the letter to his sister and

began pawing through the myriad bits of paper on his desk.

"Harris? The man who tried to ruin you?" Penny's voice seemed to come from far away.

He nodded as he continued to scrabble about the desk, tossing pens and notes about. Grabbing what appeared to be a pile of correspondence, he leafed through it with shaking fingers.

What did Harris want with Emily?

Finally he found a letter with writing similar to Harris's note. He ripped it open.

McAllister,

I hope you are satisfied. My practice is in ruins, and I am the laughingstock of London. My wife has abandoned me and what few clients I had left are trying to cancel their contracts. I would have stopped spreading the lies, but you would not let it rest at that. Your revenge has destroyed me, and I demand compensation. Perhaps a notice of your own in the newspapers, explaining that this was all a mistake. Perhaps a few of your own commissions tossed my way — I do good work, if anyone would give me the chance.

Duncan could barely read the paper

through the red haze of rage that seemed to fill the room. The scoundrel had nearly ruined Duncan's business, and he demanded Duncan's *help* in return? And had done God knows what to Emily?

He was up from his desk and out the door before he had even finished reading the letter, shouting for his horse to be saddled.

"What is it, Duncan?" Penny followed him.

He scanned the rest of the note.

Reply as soon as you receive this. I am running out of time.

Harris

"I am not certain, but I mean to find out," Duncan said, pulling on his coat. Seizing his hat from the hall table, he ran through the house to the stable yard.

Fifteen

Emily clenched her hands together in her lap. "If you want to speak to Mr. McAllister, you will have to do so directly."

"He will not answer my letters." Mr. Harris had been sitting in her salon for fifteen minutes, and in that period he had not made one shred of sense.

"I have told you. His daughter has been very ill. I doubt he has even seen his correspondence for days."

"That is a poor excuse. He is just ignoring me. He wants to ruin me!"

Emily shrank back in her chair. The man had a wild light in his eyes.

"I can send a note to Mr. McAllister and ask him to come right away."

"I thought you just said he is not reading his correspondence?" He slapped his hand on the arm of the Queen Anne chair. "There — I have caught you. Everyone lies! But I am the only one forced to confess his lies in the press."

"I was not lying. His daughter just recovered this morning. I am sure he is catching up on his paperwork at this very moment."

"So you say. But perhaps he is not. We will see. I just sent him a note myself. Perhaps he will answer this one, now that he knows I have come to visit his dear Lady Tuncliffe."

"I am not his dear anything." Perhaps if she could convince this man that she and Duncan were just friends, he would leave her in peace. Once he was gone, she could figure out what to do to keep him from returning, or from harassing Duncan further.

Emily willed her shaking hands to be still.

"If you are not his bit of muslin, then why did you lie — see, you lied again! — when you came to visit me? Why did you give me a false name?"

"Because I knew that if I gave you my real name, you would connect me to Lord and Lady Langdon, and then you would not tell me the tale about their conservatory."

"I might also have connected you to Simon. I see you have lost no time in finding a protector, and poor old Simon barely in the ground."

Emily clenched her teeth and decided not to rise to the bait. "How did you find out my real name, and link me to Mr. McAllister?"

"I am not as lacking in wit as everyone seems to think. At the theater last week, I happened to see you and mentioned to my companion that 'Mrs. Lewis' had been to my office. He happened to know your real name, and also recognized the flame-haired chit next to you as McAllister's sister. Then I found out that he had supervised the renovation of your house — the renovation you supposedly wanted me to do. Too bad about that — I tried to divert most of McAllister's clients, but I missed a few, including you. And Sherrington, for that matter. Anyway, after I learned all that, it took nothing to deduce how McAllister learned the source of the rumors."

Emily's heart sank. Duncan had been right. She had been very, very foolish to visit this man.

But what was she to do now? Suddenly, she had an idea.

"You say you want Mr. McAllister to print a retraction of your apology?"

"It is the least he owes me, after the way he has forced me to publicly ruin my own reputation. I would buy the notice myself, under his name, but he would only deny it."

Emily bit her tongue. The man was

clearly irrational, so she had little hope of engaging him in debate.

"I know a better way to redeem your reputation."

Harris's pale gray eyebrows shot up. "Go on."

Emily tried to remember all the details of a conversation she had had with Dr. Kerr while he was examining Susannah. "I happen to know of a small hospital on the western fringe of London that is looking to expand, but its funds are meager. The doctor who runs it is hoping to convince some professionals to donate their time and expertise to the project."

Harris sneered. "You want me to work for free? How will that help me pay my bills?"

Emily willed herself not to run out of patience. "Charity work does wonders for redeeming one's reputation."

"A reputation that McAllister ruined!"

She lost the battle with herself. "No, you ruined it yourself, with your lies and spite! You cannot blame Mr. McAllister for this. He is the soul of gentlemanly behavior."

"Ah, so you are enamored of the upright Scot!" He slapped his hand against the side of the chair in a random beat. "Wallace always said you were a cold one

— he talked me senseless one night, complaining about you — but it seems he was wrong. Mayhap you are simply fonder of architects than gin-sozzled viscounts. If so, you might have some warmth left for a poor, ruined Clerkenwell architect like me." Rising from his seat, he crossed the room and laid a damp hand on her bare forearm.

Emily leaped from her chair like a scalded cat and picked up a cloisonné figurine from the mantelpiece. She was not afraid of the desiccated little man; she was surrounded by servants and could probably knock him cold with the figurine if necessary. But enough was enough. "Gertie!" she bellowed, heedless of propriety.

But it was not Gertie who answered her summons. Footsteps pounded up the stairs, and moments later Duncan ran into the room.

"Emily!" he cried, rushing over to her. "Are you all right?"

"Yes, I am well," she answered calmly. "Mr. Harris was just leaving."

"I certainly was not." Harris looked at Duncan with undisguised contempt. "I knew my little note this afternoon would prompt Sir Galahad to thunder in on his white horse. He has a history of such behavior."

"Only when confronted with certain individuals."

"You can insult me all you like. I could not care less. At least I now have your attention."

"And what do you want to do with it?" Duncan's face was murderous. Emily had to give Mr. Harris credit for not turning tail and running at the sight of it.

"It is as I said in my note. You will either willingly submit a retraction to the newspapers, or you will give me some work. Both, preferably."

"If you think I will give you so much as a used pen nib, you are delusional."

"Ah, yes, but I have the key to something you value. Something you value very much."

"Which is?" Duncan advanced on the man.

"Your own good reputation."

"You can do nothing more to it. No one would believe you now."

"Before I just had stories. Today, I can have proof."

"Stop talking in riddles, man."

Harris's mouth widened in a parody of a gleeful smile. "A friend of mine is up on the roof of this house, at this moment. Give me what I want, or he will take some gin-soaked rags from his bag, touch them to a lighted lantern he carries, and stuff them down the kitchen chimney. A roaring chimney fire in Berkeley Square, in a house you renovated, will not enhance your precious reputation. It will not do much for the lovely Lady Tuncliffe's property values, either, now that I think on it."

"You are mad." Emily hardly recognized the harsh sound of her own voice. But when she spoke, Harris turned his intense attention from Duncan and trained it once again on her.

His dead gray eyes made her shiver.

Harris did not even see Duncan's swift blow to his temple coming. Instantly, he crumpled to the carpet, and Duncan moved to place his polished boot in the small of the other man's back.

"Gertie!" This time it was Duncan's turn to bellow. His shout was much louder than Emily's had been. "Gertie!"

While he was shouting, Emily moved to the windows and removed one of the long strips of fabric that secured the draperies to the wall. Wordlessly, she handed it to Duncan, who used it to bind Mr. Harris's hands behind his back.

While he was engaged in this task, Gertie ran into the room, puffing. "Yes, Mr. McAllister?"

"Go out to the mews and look up on the roof. If you see a man there, ask the grooms to bring a ladder, and then come and tell me. Please hurry."

"Yes, sir," said Gertie, not blinking an eye at this unusual request, nor at the unusual position of Emily's guest on the floor. She did, however, leave with unusual haste.

Harris groaned. "I could charge you with assault."

"I could charge you with attempted arson and have you transported," Duncan replied.

"You would not."

"I would. You keep saying your reputation is ruined. I hear they need new buildings in Van Diemen's Land, and they are none too particular about who designs them." Duncan crossed his arms across his chest.

"Ha! You can talk all you like, but I will have the last laugh! There is no arsonist on the roof." Mr. Harris twisted his head to look up at Duncan.

"I thought as much."

"You liar! You sent people to look."

"It doesn't hurt to be safe. But I had a hunch you were lying." Duncan's smile was without mirth.

"So much for your plans to transport me." Mr. Harris struggled to rise, but Duncan bent over and pinned the smaller man's shoulders down with his hands. Mr. Harris turned his head back to face the floor.

"So here is my second plan," Duncan said. "You will agree to see a doctor with the power to admit you to Bethlehem Hospital."

"Bedlam? But I am not insane!"

"That is a matter of debate."

"I will not do it!" Nigel Harris pounded his fist on the carpet.

"Well, then there is the third solution: I will challenge you for the slur to my reputation."

Emily gasped.

"Duels are illegal." Mr. Harris's voice was triumphant.

"I have no intention of dueling with you. I had more of a prizefight in mind." Duncan's voice was calm and unruffled, as though he was discussing a routine business contract.

"A prizefight?"

"Yes, at Gentleman Jackson's. If I win, I

get my reputation back."

"And if I win?"

Duncan considered. "You will have my house."

This ridiculous show of male one-upmanship was going to stop. Now. "Duncan, are you mad?" Emily's voice was icy.

Duncan stood, resting the tip of his boot against the prone man. "It will work," he mouthed, then placed a warning finger to his lips.

From the floor, Harris sputtered. "Solving disputes with one's fists. I should have expected little better from a wild Scot."

Duncan pressed his boot more firmly into the small of Harris's back. "I would not push this particular wild Scot, if I were you. What is your choice: Bedlam or boxing?"

Emily held her breath.

"I am not mad, so on both counts I choose Bedlam," Harris muttered. "No ethical physician will commit me, and boxing with you would be idiotic."

Emily released her pent-up breath in a whoosh.

After that, everything happened quickly. Dr. Kerr was summoned once again, along with a physician specializing in diseases of the mind. They arrived within an hour and took charge of Mr. Harris. There was great hustle and blustering, a stream of idle threats from Harris. With Duncan's help, the two doctors wrestled Mr. Harris into a strange armless garment called a strait-jacket, which had recently been designed for violent lunatics. Supporting the raving architect between them, they departed.

Then, all was quiet.

"Emily, I am so sorry to have put you in danger." Now that the crisis was over, Duncan was raging at his lack of foresight.

"Duncan, how could you have predicted this? Please, you have to stop blaming yourself for all the world's ills." Emily appeared remarkably serene, considering she had just spent the better part of the afternoon trapped in this room with a madman.

"But if I had only read the first letter . . ."

"You had more important things on your mind."

"That's no excuse."

Emily crossed the room and knelt before him. "Duncan, stop. You cannot control the entire world, and all the people in it."

"I did not say I could."

"Yes, you did. You said you should have prevented this. You said you should have prevented Susannah's fever." She paused. "You said you should have stopped Olivia from walking in the rain."

Pain stabbed through him, pain he had thought long dead and buried. "I should have! If she had not gone for that walk, she would have been alive today."

"You do not know that."

"It is likely." He gripped the arms of the worn Queen Anne chair and looked away from Emily.

"Even if that were true, what were you to do? Keep Olivia inside all her life? And what about Susannah? Will you forbid her to ever go to the park again — tell her she can never see her bunnies?"

Duncan's head was beginning to hum once more. "Stop it! Is it wrong to protect the people I love?"

"No. But you must let them live, as well. And you must accept that, sometimes, Providence takes them away for reasons we do not understand."

"Not if I can help it." He knew he sounded like a mulish child, but he had to make Emily understand.

"Sometimes you cannot help it." Emily reached out and squeezed his forearm. "That is the risk you must take. That is life."

Duncan leaned back in his chair. Images swirled in his mind's eye. Susannah flushed with fever. Olivia dripping in the rain. Emily's face when Harris threatened to burn down her house.

"Are you sorry you married Olivia, even though she died?" Emily asked.

He shook his head. That was one of the few truths in his life of which he was certain.

"Are you sorry that you had Susannah, even though you almost lost her?"

Duncan shook his head again. "And I'm nae sorry I met you, even though I nearly broke my neck getting here today."

Once he started to speak, the words poured out in a rush. "I was drawn to you long before I kissed you that day in the studio. I thought you were safe, and I enjoyed your company. Winning your affection became a game. If I succeeded, I thought simply that we would rub along well together. We would be good companions, but no more."

As he said the words, he realized what a foolish idea it had been. Why had he thought he could maintain a safe distance from Emily? He should have known from their first meeting — when he had been captivated by her intelligence, her sense of humor, even her violet perfume — that safety would be impossible.

He took a deep breath. "When Susannah fell ill, everything about the day Olivia died came back to me. I thought I had put that anguish behind me, with my work and my absurd jokes. But I had not, and I had no desire to go through it again. So I decided to walk away from you, before you became too dear to me."

He gave her a sheepish grin. Lifting her hand, he clasped it between both of his own. "But this afternoon, I realized it was too late for that. I love you, Emily. It frightens me, but I cannae stop."

Emily had to hug herself to keep from breaking down.

"Are you still scared?" she asked, willing her voice to be steady.

He nodded. "But I hear that is part of life."

Emily nodded. Unshed tears burned behind her eyes.

"Emily, I know you are fond of me," he began.

She cut him off. "I am much, much more than fond."

"Then why are you holding back? I thought at first it was Simon. Then, until we uncovered Mr. Harris, I thought it was my lack of prospects."

"You thought I discouraged you because your business was in trouble?" Astonishment threaded its way through her misery. "Truly, Duncan, it did not even occur to me to worry about that in the long term. I knew your practice would revive."

"If that is not the reason, then what is it?" His voice was encouraging, and she longed to confide in him. "I have bared my soul to you, Emily. Whatever your concern, it cannot be so unspeakable."

The tears spilled out now. "It is."

"Tell me." He smiled. "As you keep telling me, you will feel better."

After all they had been through together, the very least she owed him was honesty.

"I am barren," she whispered.

There, it was out. And her lovely idyll with Duncan McAllister was over. She felt his strong arms about her, and her sobs came in earnest.

"I am sorry, Duncan. I should not have led you on."

"Shhh. You didn't lead me on. In fact, you did everything to discourage me short of shooting me."

"But my efforts did not discourage you."

He chuckled. "No, they did not. And neither does this news."

She leaned back and looked at him. He did not seem distraught. In fact, his hazel eyes were warmer than she had ever seen them.

"You must know, Emily, that this does not come as a surprise to me. After all, you were married for five years."

Emily sighed. "You are right. Of course, everyone in the world probably knows. I suppose I just needed to pretend that they did not, so that it wouldn't tear at me so."

He hugged her tighter. "But why were you so afraid that this news would drive me away?"

"I have seen you with Susannah, how much you adore her." Emily's voice was flat and tired.

"Yes, I love Susannah."

"And I know that you would love to have more children."

"If that happened, I would be happy. But if it did not, it would not be the end of the world."

"You say that now." How often had she heard people say things they later regretted, make promises they could not keep?

Duncan leaned back and grasped her shoulders. "Did you not just tell me that there are things we cannot control, and that we must leave them to Providence? I could marry any woman and she could be unable to have bairns. It is the risk we take. It is part of life."

He was repeating her very words. Hoist with her own petard.

"But I do not want any woman," he continued. "I want you."

It was so tempting to stay within the comfort of his words, his embrace. But she couldn't. Slowly she extricated herself from him and stood. "Simon said I was a useless wife, that I was a —"

"Shhh. A medical fact does not make you more or less of a woman, or more or less of a wife. Anyone who says otherwise is an ass." He smiled. "Dinnae I tell you before that Simon Wallace was an ass?"

"And did I not tell you that I will think as I want, no matter what you say?"

"I know it, lass. But I will try not to order you about, I promise. If I do, you have the backbone now to put me in my place."

She thought about it. As Clare had said, any relationship was a balance of give and take, push and pull. She had not had the courage to hold up her end of the bargain with Simon. But she was a different person now than she had been as a nineteen-year-old bride.

"Emily, I am willing to take the risk that we may never have children. I am even willing to take the risk that something may happen to you before I am ready to handle it, God forbid. Are you willing to take the risk that you can overcome my overbearing tendencies?"

Could she make the leap she had urged him to make?

His voice was encouraging, seductive, enticing. "Take the chance with me, Emily. Marry me."

A slow smile spread across her face as she realized Duncan McAllister had finally released her from the prison Simon's hateful words and behavior had built. "Aye, Mr. McAllister. I dinnae know if you will be sorry, but I will chance it," she said as she fell into his arms.

Epilogue

Two years later

Duncan clenched the back of the chaise longue as another cry cracked through the house in Berkeley Square.

"How did you bear this feeling of utter helplessness, when Penny was confined?" he asked his brother-in-law, seated on the other side of the salon.

Rossley put down his port. "I didn't. I left the house and walked all the way to Southwark."

"You probably felt better the next morning than I did," said the Earl of Langdon with a rueful grin. "I finished the better part of two decanters of brandy the night our child arrived."

Duncan paced the circumference of the room for perhaps the twentieth time. "I do not remember being this distraught when Susannah was born."

Rossley looked at Langdon before replying. "You've been through a great deal since then, and you realize what can happen — better than either of us does.

But there is nothing you can do. And Emily is strong as a horse, for all that she looks like a porcelain doll."

Duncan collapsed in a chair. "The irony is, we had thought she was unable to conceive."

"Perhaps the fault lay with Simon Wallace," Langdon said.

"But is it not the general wisdom that the problem in such cases lies with the woman?" Duncan asked.

"General wisdom is often wrong. If you want more insight into women's ills, you will have to ask someone other than I." Langdon's gruff, embarrassed voice closed the topic to further discussion.

Another agonized cry filtered down from the upper story, where Clarissa and Penny were attending Emily's lying in.

"For the love of God," Duncan spat. "If I stay here any longer, I will go mad. I believe I will follow your example, Rossley, and go for a walk. To Gentleman Jackson's."

He was in the foyer putting on his hat when Gertie came down the stairs.

"Where do you think you are going, Mr. McAllister?"

"Out for a walk." He moved toward the door. He was in no mood for idle chatter.

"But there's a little boy upstairs who is

quite eager to meet his father."

Duncan turned, took one look at the little housemaid's face, and hurtled up the stairs like a steeplechaser. He doubted he touched more than two or three of the steps.

Emily's bedroom was dark and cool. In the dimness, he saw the bare outline of her beloved picture of the washerwoman; even though she now accepted painting commissions regularly, she remained adamant that this painting should hang here, far from the public eye.

"You have to let me win a battle occasionally," she often told her husband. "It keeps my hopes up."

As his vision adjusted to the weak light, he saw Emily propped up in the bed. Her hair was in wild disorder, and her eyes were ringed with deep shadows. But she was smiling. And in her arms, wrapped in a white linen cloth, was a tiny, squalling mass.

"Would you like to meet the newest member of Clan McAllister?" she said as he sat beside her on the bed. "He appears to be a bit stubborn — he took his sweet time to arrive."

"Stubborn, you say?" Duncan smiled as he kissed his wife. "I may be wrong — it happens sometimes — but I believe the wee lad will fit right in around here."

We hope you have enjoyed this Large Print book. Other Thorndike, Wheeler or Chivers Press Large Print books are available at your library or directly from the publishers.

For more information about current and upcoming titles, please call or write, without obligation, to:

Publisher
Thorndike Press
295 Kennedy Memorial Drive
Waterville, ME   04901
Tel. (800) 223-1244

Or visit our Web site at:
www.gale.com/thorndike
www.gale.com/wheeler

OR

Chivers Large Print
published by BBC Audiobooks Ltd
St James House, The Square
Lower Bristol Road
Bath BA2 3SB
England
Tel. +44(0) 800 136919
email: bbcaudiobooks@bbc.co.uk
www.bbcaudiobooks.co.uk

All our Large Print titles are designed for easy reading, and all our books are made to last.